Back to the World

Joe Campolo, Jr.

Library of Congress Control Number: 2016939204

ISBN: 978-1-943267-11-8-Trade paperback

Cover design and layout by Joyce Faulkner

Printed in the United States.

What People are Saying ...

Back to the World is a well crafted follow-up to *The Kansas NCO*. Joe Campolo allows the reader to experience the frustrations of returning Vietnam veterans whose country abandoned them. Joe is able to take you from the jungles of Nam to the mean streets of America. God Bless all our veterans.

~ George Dooley, U.S. Air Force, Vietnam era veteran

Once in a great while, a reader will come across a book that is so engaging and captivating it is very difficult to put down. *Back to the World*, by Joe Campolo Jr. is such a book. The author is a superb storyteller; the book is a fast paced suspense thriller. Great job, Mr. Campolo!

~ John Podlaski, Vietnam War veteran and author of *Cherries: A Vietnam War Novel*

In *Back to the World*, Cru and his buddies have survived their life-threatening experiences in Vietnam, but their return to the "World" has not gone as smoothly as expected. In a fast-paced sequel to *The Kansas NCO*, we get to see how Andrew Crucianelli and his crew deal with a country that has little regard for their post-war future.

~ Dick Evenson, writer, retired marketing executive, and U.S. Army artillery veteran

Joe Campolo has hit another home run with *Back to the World*! This fast-paced thriller keeps you on the edge of your seat as it follows the trail of two vigilantes challenging the Mob.

~ Bob Doerr, award winning author of the Jim West mysteries

This book is dedicated to my children,

Billy and JoAnn,

and to my grandchildren

John and Lucy.

And also to the memory of my best friend,

Jim Booth

Prologue

It had been six months since Doug Montrell returned from his tour of duty in Vietnam. Back in Nam, it was Montrell's idea to go on the mission that resulted in the death of his best friend, Terry Hardy. The two were initially excused from the mission, but Montrell volunteered anyway. And Hardy would not let Montrell go alone, a decision that cost him his life.

The mission was a setup by Howard McKay, a senior non-commissioned officer who'd gone rogue. McKay worked for William E. Richards, a man known as the Kansas NCO. Richards ran what was possibly the largest black market operation of the Vietnam War, and while his black market operations were focused on money exchange, NCO club operations, and other such scams, his underling, Howard McKay ventured into the deadly world of drugs and weapon smuggling.

Montrell was finishing out the last eighteen months of his four year U.S. Air Force commitment at Wright-Patterson Air Force Base, after recovering from wounds he also received on the lethal mission. Although he'd made plans to visit Terry Hardy's parents, he found excuse after excuse to delay the trip.

Having run out of excuses, Montrell finally made the trip to visit Mel and Marleah Hardy. On the second morning of his visit, Montrell and Terry Hardy's father were fly fishing in a nearby stream. "Should I try this Woolly Booger?" Doug asked.

Laughing, Mel Hardy told him, "No, no Woolly Buggers today, Doug. Try this Adams fly." The two fished in the morning mist of the peaceful stream until they had a full creel of brook trout. Later at the Hardy home, Terry's mother prepared them for dinner.

1

"That was great, Mrs. Hardy," Doug said after consuming three helpings of fish, homemade French fries and coleslaw.

Marleah moved them out to the porch after the dishes were done. "How are Andrew and Arnold doing?" she asked. Before his death, Terry dutifully wrote his mother every day, telling her all about their close-knit group in Vietnam.

Andrew Crucianelli and Arnold Redmond were with Terry Hardy and Doug Montrell when Terry was killed. The close-knit group found themselves fighting for their lives trying to extricate themselves from the deadly jungle where they had been targeted by both Viet Cong and Americans associated with McKay's black market operation. Montrell felt it unnecessary to burden the Hardy's with all of the intrigues which their son and his companions had dealt with.

"Cru and Red are doing okay. Cru moved out west, guessing he thinks he's going to be a movie star. I believe Red is still on the Ojibwa reservation where he was raised. He had hoped to go on to college to qualify for a job where he could help the underprivileged kids on the reservation."

Mel Hardy pulled on his pipe. "Good, I hope they succeed. I know a lot of you boys haven't been treated too well since you got back." As a World War II veteran, Mel understood some of the problems the returning veterans faced. "I'm ashamed to say that some members of my local VFW post haven't been too welcoming to Vietnam veterans. This damn war has put our whole country in an uproar. We've forgotten who we are...our ideals." Thinking about it angered Mel, "Never thought I'd see the day... we're turning on each other."

Marleah Hardy gently patted Mel's hand, "Don't upset yourself, honey, it's beyond our control." She changed the subject. "Doug, how are Sergeant Prentice and Hoa doing?"

Charles Prentice was the non-commissioned officer in charge of the unit their son and his friends were assigned to during their time in Vietnam. Prentice was a man with many human failings. However, he redeemed himself and came through for his men when they needed him the most. Ngyuen Than Hoa was a young Vietnamese man the group had befriended during their deadly ordeal fighting their way out of the bush. The men originally thought he was a Viet Cong. However he turned out to be just another unfortunate victim of the constant state of war his country was in. The survivors of the mission helped Hoa fulfill his dream of immigrating to the United States.

Smiling, Montrell told the Hardy's, "Sergeant Prentice is doing fine. He's finishing out his Air Force career in Georgia, says he wants to start a peanut farm when he gets out. When I last spoke with Hoa, he was working on a shrimp boat in Louisiana. He sounded happy. We all hope to get together for a reunion one of these days."

Mel nodded. "That's great. I hope you guys stay in touch. You will find that those men are the best friends you will ever have in life." Looking curious, Mel asked, "Doug...why do you guys refer to the United States as 'the world'?"

Laughing, Doug explained, "Well, Vietnam was completely foreign to us in so many ways. Not just the country and the people, but our whole way of life there. Because of the bizarre nature of the war, we even took on a totally different appearance and demeanor. It was indeed a different world. We had left the real world and entered this strange, crazy place—that we felt was just an aberration—which we would eventually leave to return to the real world... our world."

"I get it now," Mel nodded.

The three sat in peace, enjoying the cool evening breeze. As the baleful whistle of a distant train sounded, Marleah took a deep breath and quietly asked, "Did Terrence suffer badly, Doug?"

Montrell paused for a moment. "Terry died instantaneously, Mrs. Hardy. He had a look of peace when

3

he passed."

Marleah was now able to release her breath. "Thank you, Doug. Thank you." Then, as if an internal valve had been opened, she sobbed long and hard. Her husband gently held her and stroked her hand.

PART ONE

"You can't go home again."

~Thomas Wolfe

Chapter 1

"Ready for another beer, Andy?"

Andrew Crucianelli was sitting in a booth across from the bar, staring at the bubbles rising to the surface of his third glass of beer. The small tavern in North Hollywood, California, was owned by his great-aunt, who lived upstairs in a small apartment she now shared with Cru. All Aunt Tesla asked was that he sweep up at night and help out with the occasional rowdy customer.

Other than his mother, everyone called Andrew Crucianelli by his nickname Cru, and he took no notice of the bartender speaking to him, immersed in his thoughts.

"Andy?"

"Oh. Sorry, Sharon. No thanks. After this one, I'm heading out to put in an application at the GM plant."

"Well, good luck then."

After his return from Vietnam in November of 1970, Cru found few job prospects back home in Wisconsin. His Air Force training as a supply clerk was of little use to any of the employers in the area.

"I'm heading out west," he told his parents after two months of fruitless searching.

His father thought it was foolish. "Have you tried Snap-On Tools? They're always hiring."

"They said I wasn't qualified, and they didn't have the time to train anyone."

"Dynamatic?" his dad prodded.

Andy grimaced. "They have an unwritten policy not to hire Vietnam vets. Guess they think we're all drug-crazed killers."

This angered Cru's father. "Those sons of bitches! How about American Brass?"

Cru was shaking his head. "Not qualified, not qualified, not qualified."

Sighing, Cru's mother was pragmatic. "Well, then you should do what you feel you need to do, Andy. You know Aunt Tesla would welcome you anytime. You could probably stay with her until you catch on somewhere." She was trying to sound cheerful.

Smiling, Cru agreed. "When I become president of a Hollywood film studio, get a good tan, and buy a home in Beverly Hills with an Olympic-sized swimming pool, I'll send for you, Mom."

But after a month in California, it was apparent it would be quite some time before Cru would be moving into that Beverly Hills home. During his time in Vietnam, Cru went through hell. He always said if he lived through that, nothing would ever bother him again, but now he was bothered. And frustrated.

He returned from his trip to the auto plant angry, and threw himself into a corner booth in his aunt's little tavern.

Sharon set a cold beer down in front of him. "This one's on me."

"Thanks, Sharon. You'll have to wait for your heavenly reward, though. Looks like I'm destined for a life of poverty. Or crime."

"Hey, why not make it easy on yourself, GI?" The man in the next booth moved into Cru's booth and sat across from him.

Surprised, Cru looked up and recognized the man as a fellow veteran who attended night classes with him at Los Angeles Valley College, a community college in the San Fernando Valley. They spoke over coffee on occasion, finding common ground in their mutual background of military service in Vietnam.

"Hey, Tibbits. What the hell you doing here? There ain't no mama-sans around here to harass."

"And that's a damn shame because there's nothing like a hot mama-san and a cold beer after a day's work."

"At least you found work. I can't even get a job shining shoes at the airport."

Recalling that Tibbits lived on the opposite side of the San Fernando Valley, Cru was curious. "Straying kind of far tonight, aren't you, Tibbits?"

"Say! You like hot food?" Tibbits changed the subject. Before Cru could reply, Tibbits said, "Hell, you're a dago, course you do. Let's take a ride. There's a great little Mexican cantina down the road with an outdoor pavilion where we can talk."

Cru asked Sharon to tell his aunt he wouldn't make it home for supper and kept an eye on Tibbits as they walked out of the bar.

Tibbits laughed. "This ain't a fucking hit, so don't be so suspicious, you hardheaded dago."

Before Tibbits could take another step, Cru spun him around and threw him onto the pavement. "We've already established that I'm a dago and that I'm suspicious. You better tell me where we're going and why. Like right now, my friend."

With a look of surprise, Tibbits held his hands up. "Easy. Easy, man, I'm just busting your balls. Didn't mean to piss you off. Let's get to that cantina and have some tequila. I got a plan I think you might want to get in on."

Letting him up, Cru said, "Fine, but before we move along let's get one thing straight. I don't take shit off of anybody, and I'm nobody's fool. You better not be jerking my chain."

Cru and Tibbits sat in the cantina pavilion sipping tequila and listening to the mariachi band. One of the guitarists was the owner of the cantina and the other two were his brothers.

"I like this music," Cru commented, listening to the melodic guitars and daydreaming. He wondered if his buddies from Vietnam—Arnold Redmond and Doug Montrell—were faring any better than he was. "Sorry for the dust-up back there. Since coming back from Nam, I'm as jumpy as a monkey fucking a football."

"I hear you, brother. It ain't easy being around all these civilians, listening to them whine about their cars, or what they gonna do for Thanksgiving, or how their girlfriends won't blow them, or whatever."

"Yeah." Three shots, and Cru was already getting a case of the ass, his anger building. He didn't like civilians too damn much at this point, either. The memory of his return from Vietnam was still fresh in his mind. Those people in Seattle were unbelievable, greeting the returning men with a barrage of garbage. To rub salt in the wound, the local VFW in his hometown locked the Vietnam vets out. Cru was in a bitter frame of mind, and the tequila was only sharpening his anger. Of late, Cru often found himself wondering how Red and his other friends from the Nam were making out.

* * *

"God dammit, net that fish, boy!"

Arnold Redmond grabbed the landing net from the back of the boat and deftly scooped up the walleye for one of the clients he was guiding on the remote Canadian lake.

Red had returned to his home on the White Earth Indian Reservation in Northern Minnesota as soon as he completed his tour of duty in Vietnam. Finding few prospects on the reservation, he spent most of his time drinking with his cousin, Daniel Lightfeather.

"I'm telling you Red, we could make some decent money at the fishing lodge up by Eagle Lake. A hundred and fifty a week plus tips. And all the fish we can eat."

Thinking it was better than turning into another reservation drunk, Red signed on as a guide at the small fishing lodge where he and Daniel handled the boat, netted and cleaned all the fish, and did anything else the clients of the lodge required of them.

It was now August and Red had been a guide at the lodge for about two months. Most of the time he didn't mind the work, and he even made enough money to send some to his mother back on the reservation. This week Red was guiding for a pair of men he didn't particularly like. They ordered him around like a cabin boy and made crude remarks about his ancestry. By noon they were usually too drunk to fish, but insisted that Red catch enough fish to fill out their quota.

On this particular day, the two men fished and drank until noon, then passed out. Red fished the remainder of the day.

"We're back at the lodge now," he told the groggy men upon their return.

The men were slow to stir and woke up in a surly mood, complaining about the fish.

"What the fuck did you keep these puny little runts for?" the larger of the two demanded.

"It was a slow day. I couldn't have filled out your tags without them. They're legal."

"Well I ain't paying for 'em, and I ain't paying you, you dumbfuck heathen," the man raged.

Red shrugged. "I don't give a fuck what you do with the fish, but the lodge pays me whether you like it or not."

"If they pay you for this shit, I'll stiff 'em," the man huffed.

Stepping onto the pier, Red shrugged. "Do what you want."

As Red reached into the boat for his gear, the man tried to hit him with an oar.

"Get smart with me, you gut-eating bastard," the man yelled.

Red dodged the swinging oar and with a deft move

kicked the man in the sternum, sending him splashing into the cold lake. The other man jumped up and took a step toward Red, who spun around and kicked him in the side, sending him into the water next to his friend. Sputtering and flailing, the two drunks started yelling and cussing up a storm. Red gathered up his gear, cursed the two men thrashing around in the water, and went up to his cabin.

Within fifteen minutes, the lodge owner was pounding on his door.

Chapter 2

In the small cantina, Bob Tibbits explained his plan to Cru in detail, hoping to entice him into partnering up. "You know how we always bitch about that asshole Tito at the university?" Tibbits asked.

Cru frowned. "Yeah, that Mexican fuck is getting rich selling drugs to all those worthless hippies and college punks."

"That's right, and I figure on getting in on some of that."

"Well, I sure as hell didn't see that job posting in the want ads. Anyway, I don't think Tito's an equal opportunity employer, Bob."

Nodding his head, Tibbits said, "That's right, my friend. I'm sure he's not, but my intention is not to work for Tito. My intention is in letting Tito do the work, then relieving him of the profits."

Now Tibbits had Cru's attention. "You're going to rob him?"

"Him and all the other dealers in the area. You don't like those assholes any more than I do, and it's apparent that you could use the money."

Cru wasn't so sure. "Yeah, sure I could use the money, and yeah, I hate the drug dealing slime, but that doesn't mean I'm gonna start a war with these lowlifes. For each one we see, there are at least a dozen backing him up. And some are hooked up with Mexican drug gangs, not to mention the mob. I just got back from Nam where I almost got my ass shot off more than once. I'm not looking for another Purple Heart."

Tibbits raised his hand in acknowledgement. "I hear you, brother. If you recall, I recently came back from that same shit hole. I'm not taking any unnecessary chances on getting my ass greased either. Listen to my plan—hear me out, okay?"

After Tibbits filled in the details, Cru sat silent for several minutes sucking on his tequila sour. "There's a guy I know who is very good at this type of shit. A natural born Green Beret and a guy I trust with my life. If Red agrees to go in on it, I'm in. I'll let you know."

With the prospect of adventure, Cru felt like a man with a goal; he felt alive again. He hadn't had that feeling since he was fighting his way out of the jungles in Vietnam.

* * *

"Why don't you come out here and join us?" Cru asked.

"Who exactly is 'us'?" Red wanted to know.

Red had returned from Canada where he was terminated from his job at the fishing lodge. The lodge owner, while sympathetic to the circumstances, could not allow his clients to be physically assaulted by the staff, right or wrong.

Cru picked Redmond up at the Los Angeles International Airport two weeks later.

"Good flight?"

Smiling, Red nodded. "Not bad at all. There was a cute little stewy who gave me free drinks all the way. LA is her home base."

"And you got her number, you old dog?"

"Damn straight! But I'm thinking that with robbing drug dealers and shit, you must be flush with cash and hot babes yourself," Red probed.

"You know I wouldn't start a gig without my old partner."

Red laughed. "Damn, you mean we're cherries again?

Cru nodded. "Tomorrow night's our first mission.

We'll head over to my partner's place and go over the plan and all the details. We can burn a steak on his grill and have a few beers."

"How well do you know this dude? Do you trust him?"

"Trust him about as much as I can. He's an Army vet, got back from Nam about six months before we did. We both go to night classes at Los Angeles Valley College. We're in a couple of the same classes together."

"They let your ass in a damn university?"

Laughing, Cru said, "Damn straight. They even elected me as a community outreach coordinator!"

"The cat in the fucking hen house!" Red thought that was hilarious. "Let's get moving. I'm ready for that beer."

* * *

Cru, Red, and Tibbits eased into the darkened east parking lot at the community college. Tibbits drove a standard four-door sedan, and Cru drove an old junker. After noting where Tibbits parked, Cru drove to the west parking lot and left his vehicle there.

The three men met in the center of the outdoor mall, which saw the heaviest foot traffic of the campus. They quietly moved to their predetermined positions, concealed but affording them a panoramic view of the surroundings.

At the center of the mall next to a large shrubby area stood Tito. Now and then, a passerby would approach Tito, and a transaction would take place. Tito's wares included LSD, marijuana, Thai stick, and amphetamines, as well as depressants known as reds. He engaged in a thriving business at the college and, thanks to the threat of retribution from his bosses, no competitors encumbered the lucrative commerce he enjoyed.

Around eleven o'clock, business slowed down. Tito, who frequently took a pull from the flask in his rear pocket, walked behind the shrubs to urinate. As he relieved himself, he thought he heard something, but before he could turn and check, Cru eased up behind him and smacked him on the side of the head with a small leaded slapjack. Tito went down like a box of rocks, whereby Cru and Tibbits relieved him of his money and remaining drugs. Red kept watch from his nearby post, ensuring that no one observed or interrupted the operation.

"Okay, let's get the fuck out of here," Cru called in a loud whisper.

"Hang on," Tibbits said, and proceeded to urinate on Tito, who was still out cold.

Laughing hysterically, Tibbits zipped up his pants, and the three moved off to their respective vehicles to drive back to Tibbits's apartment.

* * *

"This is bullshit!" Alton Deem had worked himself into a lather. "Five rip-offs in less than two months, and you assholes expect me to believe that one of you—or all of you—aren't in on it?"

Tito and nine other men were standing silently in a warehouse near LAX being grilled by their boss.

Alton Deem was one of the largest Anglo drug suppliers left in Southern California, and until recently, his operation had run smoothly and unimpeded. Deem had built his drug business from the ground up after dropping out of high school and starting a lucrative business by supplying his former classmates.

"These guys have boosted me for damn near twenty large in cash and at least that much in drugs," Deem raged. "You fucks have been living like a bunch of goddamn kings: cash, whores, cars, dope. All the while, I'm getting robbed! Well now the cushy life is ending. I'm giving you one week to come up with something."

"Pardon, el jefe," one of the men spoke up, "but we have been hunting endlessly for the men who have done this. They work quickly and leave no trace. I have threatened my men with death if they are involved. I even eliminated some, as a precaution. We will not stop until we find them."

This did not placate Deem. "I don't want to hear any more of these fucking lame excuses. This ain't the goddamn Peace Corps. This shit doesn't get taken care of, there will be some permanent changes in management. Now get the fuck out of here."

Tito and several of the others stopped at a nearby strip club. They sat in their favorite seats at the bar, nursing their drinks and idly watching the bored dancer in front of them. She had gone through three dances and only picked up seven dollars in tips from the group of morose men who were watching. Finally, one of the men said, "Someone's gonna get clipped."

Nodding his head, Tito agreed. "I'll say it right now, amigos. I find out who's in on this shit, I'll cut his balls off myself...and the balls of his firstborn male child if he has one. You guys know anything, you better start talking."

Chapter 3

"Let's nail this prick," Cru said.

Cru, Red, and Tibbits were sitting in their sedan near the Greyhound station in downtown Los Angeles. It was midnight and they were watching Monk, who was standing near a phone booth, selling drugs.

"Let's just wait a bit." Red was in a pensive mood. "Kind of strange running into Lopez at Ralph's today."

"Yeah," said Cru, "but it was good to see him again, that big ugly bastard. Didn't recognize him out of uniform. I wasn't aware he was from this area."

Victor Manuel Lopez was a sergeant major in the First Cavalry unit of the Army when Crucianelli and Redmond met him in Vietnam. Lopez had played an important role in saving Red, Cru, and some others who were caught up in a black market heroin smuggling operation. They'd bumped into him in the parking lot of the large food chain earlier that day, exchanged greetings, and talked about getting together some time.

"I get to nail the bastard this time, right?" Tibbits wanted to know. He wasn't interested in the conversation about Lopez and wanted to be sure it was his turn with the slapjack. "You guys have all the fun. I'm just the damn delivery boy in this outfit. "It ain't right, seeing as how it was my idea in the first place."

Cru said, "Yeah, yeah, I said you could this time, didn't I?"

"And I'm still pissing on him after you get the money and drugs," Tibbits said.

18

"I don't really get why you think that's cool, even though they're dirt bags. Besides as much beer as you've been drinking, it'd probably take you fifteen minutes. We don't have that kind of time."

Red wasn't taking part in the joking today. He'd had an uneasy feeling ever since they'd arrived a couple hours earlier.

Noticing Red's mood, Cru prodded him. "What's the matter, Red? That cockpit cutie cut you off?"

Red kept looking around, scanning for anything out of place.

"Something's up," he said.

Cru and Tibbits got quiet and started looking around as well. After a minute Cru spoke up.

"You see something, Red?"

"Haven't seen anything, just sensing something wrong here." Red kept scanning the area with one of the night scopes they'd acquired.

"Must have been some bad frijoles," Tibbits said. "I don't see anything."

"You couldn't see your dick if your hand was tied to it. Can't believe you made it through the Nam," Cru chided.

"Hey man, I was a lean mean fighting machine!"

"The key word is 'was'," said Crucianelli. "I'd say you better sign up for another tour. Looks like you've packed on about twenty pounds just since I've known you."

"Guys, I think we should pass on this one tonight," Red interrupted.

Cru thought about it, then looked over at Tibbits. "If Red ain't okay with this, I say we abort the mission."

Tibbits, however, did not want to pass on an opportunity so close at hand. "Look guys, we've scoped this one out for the last three days. We've been watching almost two hours tonight and nothing's changed. This asshole Monk is standing over there with at least three grand in his pocket just for the taking. I don't feel like going home with nothing to show for the trip."

After a short time, Cru looked over at Red. "Red?"

"I told you what I thought. You guys still want to move on it, I'll do my part, but something's up, I tell you."

Cru thought hard for a few moments. "Okay, we do it, but goddammit, we do it quick. And we keep our eyes everywhere. No wasted time pissing on the asshole or any of that shit. We knock him cold, grab the cash, and get the fuck outta here."

"What about the drugs?" Tibbits didn't want to concede anything of value.

Cru gave him a firm look. "We grab the fucking cash and di di mau!" He used the Vietnamese term for "go" to emphasize his point.

Crucianelli and Tibbits approached the phone booth where Monk was standing. Redmond stood behind a nearby vendor kiosk where he could observe the surrounding area. Just as they got into position behind Monk, Tibbits stepped on some broken glass. Monk wheeled around sharply and Tibbits panicked, lunging at him and flailing away with the slapjack. Not seriously hurt, Monk put up a struggle and started yelling.

"Fuck!" Cru grunted as he stepped in behind Monk, grabbed him, and covered his mouth. "Whack him good!" he ordered Tibbits, who kept beating Monk until he went limp. Cru let him go and he slipped onto the ground. Having watched this performance, Red scanned the area as he ran over to render assistance. He was moving in when he saw three men in a nearby alley running toward their position.

"Bandits! Bandits at two o'clock!" Red yelled. He pulled out his pistol and got down into a kneeling position to cover Cru and Tibbits, who were still focused on Monk. "Go! Go! Go!" Red yelled, as he laid down cover fire.

Crucianelli immediately took off at a dead run, but Tibbits lingered. "Leave him, dammit!" Red shouted and grabbed Tibbits, who pushed him off while still trying to urinate on his unconscious victim. Needing to reload, Red took off running while still yelling at Tibbits. "Leave him! Leave him!"

Within seconds the sound of heavy automatic weapons filled the air. Looking over his shoulder Red saw Tibbits getting riddled with bullets. The impact of the rounds kept him vertical for several seconds, arms flailing like a scarecrow in a gale. Red started to turn and go back to help, but the attackers quickly raised their aim. Red could only watch in horror as Tibbits's head exploded like a watermelon hit by a sledge hammer.

One of the attackers yelled, "Get that other bastard!"

But getting Red would not be easy. Fleet of foot, Red put distance between him and the men who attacked them. He ran a zigzag pattern for fifteen minutes before reaching the fall-back car where Cru was waiting.

"Tibbits?" Cru asked, though he feared he knew the answer.

Red just shook his head as he jumped in the passenger seat.

Cru frowned as he motored away, eyes flicking back and forth between the road and the rearview mirror.

"Fuck," he muttered. Tibbits was a brother, a Vietnam veteran, and a friend.

Red sat rigid, looking straight ahead. "He didn't want to leave without pissing on the dude. I couldn't reload and lay cover fire fast enough. Sorry."

"Not your fault, Red. Bob knew the risks. It could happen to anyone who gets careless. We saw that enough in Nam."

"I know but I still feel bad about it. Let's fall back to our trailer and mellow out for a while."

Chapter 4

Crucianelli was feeling the pressure. After the ambush, he and Redmond moved to their small camper out in the desert near San Bernardino. Every few days, Cru went into LA to check on his apartment and go through any mail he may have received. After scouting the area, he gathered the mail and a few other belongings, then went to a park to go through the mail.

Cru opened Montrell's letter first. Doug Montrell was still a buddy, especially after being seriously wounded on that mission, the one where they had been set up by members of a black market operation. His letter said he needed to speak to Cru...urgently. They usually found time to talk on the phone once a week, even though it was a long distance call to Ohio. But the letter instructed Cru to call him at a given phone number at a specific time later that day. Cru went to a busy shopping center where he waited around, then called his friend from a pay phone at the instructed time. After a short greeting, Montrell got right to the point.

"What exactly are you guys doing out there?" he asked.

"You know we're running an import export business, Monty. I told you that before." Cru hoped to placate Montrell.

Montrell wasn't buying the smoke screen. "Okay, I'll cut right to the chase. Time may be running out for you and Red."

"What the fuck you talking about, Monty?"

Montrell raised his voice. "Cru, just shut up and listen.

When I'm done, if you still want to blow smoke, then fine. But hear me out now." After a short pause he continued. "I've got a close friend from Toledo named Vinnie. Vinnie has connections with the mob."

"Yeah, I remember you talking about him in Nam, Falcon something or other. You guys palled around when you were kids."

"Right, Vinnie Falconnetti. Well It seems a guy by the name of Alton Deem is a player in a very large drug dealing operation in Southern California, and his dealers on the street have been getting hit by a group of men using military tactics." Montrell paused. "You listening?"

"Go on."

"After weeks of getting targeted, this Deem character got a real hard-on and set up an ambush. One of the fuckers robbing them was killed, but the others got away. The guy's name was Tabbot or something like that, an ex-GI who served in Nam. Apparently he was a real operator who sent a lot of shit back home via the black market." Montrell paused again. "Have I got your attention now?"

"Sure, Monty, but where the hell you going with this?" Cru asked.

"This Tabbot character was traced to a lease on a small warehouse out near San Bernardino."

"Yeah?" Cru prodded. He wasn't ready to admit to anything yet.

"Yeah is right," Montrell said. "The cosigner on the lease is none other than someone named Andrew Crucianelli. Now it would be hard for me to believe there're two of you out there."

Montrell gave Cru a bit of time to digest everything and then added, "You want to tell me what's going on out there, Cru? Or you want to keep blowing smoke up my ass?"

Crucianelli said nothing for a time.

"Cru?" Montrell prodded.

Crucianelli realized he could no longer continue the

ruse. "All right, I'll fill you in on everything, Monty. But first you tell me how the fuck your friend came to know all this shit."

"No problem. Other than the Mexicans who are taking over, no one can work in Southern California without the explicit blessings of the mob. The mob in LA is run by the Dragna family. One of Vinnie's cousins who moved out there happens to work for them now. He keeps his ear to the ground and keeps Vinnie up to date on anything of interest. The Dragnas have been losing ground to the Mexican gangs and are supersensitive about being rolled by what they believe to be a bunch of amateurs."

Cru digested this information, and then revealed in detail everything that he and Red had been doing since they started their enterprise of knocking over drug dealers. He explained how they planned it, what methods they used, and how much money they had obtained.

"Wow," was all Montrell could say when Cru finished.

"Well, you're an accomplice now, Monty, so don't turn us in." Crucianelli hoped to lighten the impact.

"You can joke all you want, buddy, but you guys got some big trouble."

Now it was Cru who demanded information. "Just how did your buddy Vinnie tie all this shit to you?" That was a legitimate question. Connecting Crucianelli to Montrell, based solely on the information Vinnie Falconnetti had, appeared to be quite a reach.

"When I was recovering in that VA shit hole in Utah, two people came to visit me: my mother and Vinnie Falconnetti. The only thing I was capable of doing for a couple of months was talk, and I talked my ass off. I told Vinnie all about our little adventure in Nam. He probably knows you and Red better than your own mothers do at this point."

"I get it. And now I have to ask...do you think this information will stay with your friend?"

24

"He gave me his word. I trust Vinnie almost as much as I trust you two. You guys have to figure out how the hell you're gonna get out of this mess."

"Thanks for the heads-up, Monty. And thank your friend. We'll take care of the problem. Red and I can be pretty damn slippery, as you well know. We better cut this short. How about I send you a note to set up our next call."

"Anything I can do from my end?" Montrell asked.

"No. It's bad enough Red and I got our necks under the axe. You already put your time in at that VA hellhole. Don't want to see you back there, buddy."

Chapter 5

When Cru returned to the trailer out in the desert, he put away the supplies he'd picked up, got a cold beer out of the fridge, and waited for Red. Red was out hunting jack rabbits and hadn't returned yet. Jack rabbits flavored many of their meals when they stayed at the trailer, and Red's proficient aim with his old Remington pump .22 kept the small chest freezer nicely stocked. Today he returned with three more.

"Hey," he said, acknowledging Crucianelli, and tossed the still warm carcasses on the kitchen table. "Anything up at the apartment?"

"Hey, Red." Saying no more, Cru got a cold beer out of the fridge, gave it to Red, and sat down.

From Cru's demeanor, Red knew something was wrong. "What's up, buddy?"

"We got problems."

Red pulled on the cold beer, "Old news, brother. Tell me something I don't know."

Cru shook his head. "Let me put it this way. We've got more problems. Bigger problems."

"Bigger problems than a heavyweight drug-dealing gang trying to kill us?" Red asked.

"Oh, yeah. I got a letter from Doug Montrell. Asked me to call him at a pay phone at a specific time earlier today. Lucky I was there to get the letter in time."

"And?" Red prodded.

Cru took a long pull on his beer and then filled Red in on his conversation with their friend while Red sat quietly.

When Cru finished, Red retrieved a bottle of Jack Daniels and poured each of them a shot. "I guess we can't expect any consideration for a fellow dago from the Dragna bunch, huh?"

Laughing, Cru said, "Well, Red, even if we could, it wouldn't do you any good. You're a fucking heathen."

"Hell, you made me an honorary dago back in Nam. Remember?"

"Yeah, and you made me an honorary Ojibwa. That and fifteen cents will get us a cup of coffee anywhere in town."

Red got serious again. "I think we're going to have to relocate."

"Been thinking about that ever since I talked to Monty. First we have to figure out what we want to do and what we need. Then we'll pick out a few places and narrow it down from there. And we probably need to do it pretty quick."

* * *

"I'll nail the bastards," Alton Deem promised. Deem was in an unaccustomed position, being dressed down and threatened. Normally he was the one doing the lecturing and threatening, but not today.

"Sure you will," Louie Dragna commented derisively. He'd sent for Deem after the bungled ambush in which two of the men ripping off their drug operations had escaped right under their noses.

"We got the one. We'll nail the other two. Just give me a chance," Deem pleaded.

"You couldn't nail your hat to a wall, you cheap pimp."

Seething, Deem stood mute, unwilling to further incur the wrath of a man who was known to sew the lips of his enemies shut before beating them to death.

Louie Dragna was the muscle end of the Dragna crime family, the last Italian crime family in all of Los Angeles, including the large metropolitan area which comprised its sprawling suburbs. In addition to their criminal network, the Dragna family had holdings in many legitimate enterprises in the area. All of them were run as efficiently as any Fortune 500 company, although employee discipline could be harsh, and the retirement programs were often abrupt.

Despite those considerations, Louie's older brother Mario, who handled the legitimate end of the businesses, considered himself no different than the CEO of any other multinational corporation. So long as the profits poured in and no adverse publicity encumbered their activities, he took little notice of how Louie handled the more problematic side of the enterprise.

As word spread that the Dragna drug operation was vulnerable, even Mario hoped for the quick demise of the perpetrators who were creating doubt regarding the family's prowess. For years the powerful Mexican mafia had been making inroads into what was once the exclusive territory of the Italian Mafia. And demographics had turned the tide in the Mexicans' favor. Mario recognized this and was willing to yield the risky and violent drug business to the Mexicans, but Louie was reluctant to let go.

"You got three weeks, Deem," Louie said. "Three weeks to straighten this shit out."

"Thank you. Thank you, Mr. Dragna!" Deem gushed with relief. "You won't regret it."

"I never regret anything, Deem," Louie said, sending ice through Alton's veins. "If the faggots robbing me aren't dead at the end of three weeks, I assure you, you will be."

Chapter 6

Cru and Red closed their bank accounts, cleaned out the safe deposit boxes, and terminated the lease on their warehouse. They sent Tibbits's share of the money to his mother. Then they packed up their LA apartment and drove back to their trailer in the desert with all their possessions in a small U-Haul towed behind one of their cars, an old junker with a V-8 engine.

After considering several locations, Cru and Red had determined to move to Albuquerque, New Mexico. It was centrally located in relation to Denver, Phoenix, San Diego, and Dallas, the other cities under consideration. Their operation required a large metropolitan area with a sizable airport. They also needed a location where illegal drugs were frequently brought in from outside the country.

"Buncha damn Apaches live near Albuquerque," Redman groused from the passenger seat of the old sedan, referring to the Native Americans who would soon be neighbors of sorts.

Cru thought this was humorous. "You mean to say you're prejudiced against some of your own blood brothers, Red?"

"You should talk," Redmond shot back. "I hear you badmouthing your fellow Italians all the time."

"Well if you ain't a Sicilian or Calabrese, you ain't worth shit."

"And you call 'em all Pinocchio," Redmond added. "What's with that?"

"Finocchio. It's finocchio, Red. It means you're a Tinkerbell, light in the loafers, queer. Get it? But what have you got against the Apaches, anyway? I always liked Cochise."

"You watch too much TV, Cru. I bet you still think Captain Kangaroo was from Australia. For your information, the Apache are a bunch of damn gut-eaters, very crude people, even by Indian standards. And I didn't know you were such a damn prude about sex."

Cru chuckled, "I don't give a shit about anyone's sex habits. I just like to bust people's balls. And I bet you'd eat guts if you were starving. I'm thinking I would, too."

Though bantering back and forth, the two were on alert. Pulling the trailer, they stayed in the right lane of the freeway with the slower traffic. Red's radar suddenly went on full alert. "That black cargo van behind us got on the freeway the same time we did."

Both men looked through the side view mirrors at the heavy-duty vehicle directly behind them. Cru switched lanes and increased his speed. Soon after, the cargo van did the same.

"Shit, they're tailing us." Cru pulled back into the right lane, intending to get off at the next exit.

Red reached between the bucket seats and grabbed the sawed-off shotgun loaded with double-aught shot. The black van increased its speed and pulled alongside. The passenger window came down, and the barrel of an assault rifle slid out.

"Hit it!" Red screamed, just as the automatic weapon opened up on them.

Cru slammed the accelerator pedal to the floor, and the quad barrel, 8-cylinder sedan took off like a shot. A hail of bullets struck the rear of the car and the U-Haul trailer, blowing out the rear windows and the trailer tires. The van rapidly closed the distance, attempting to get in position to shoot again.

"Fuck you, assholes!" Cru shouted as he jerked the

steering wheel back and forth, causing the trailer to slew back and forth, slamming into the black van. The van maneuvered to avoid the swerving trailer, but got clipped several times, causing the driver to lose control.

"Hang on!" Cru shouted as he continued to maneuver.

The trailer tongue was now damaged, and the trailer itself started twisting and spinning like an alligator on a carcass. The tongue finally separated from the car, and the safety chains let go with a snap. The U-Haul careened into the black van which was swerving all over the road. Both veered off the right shoulder and down the steep embankment, tumbling over and over until they reached the bottom.

"Yes!" Red shouted, jumping up and down in his seat. "Die, you bastards!"

Nearby vehicles slowed down and stopped to check on the wreck, allowing Cru and Red to continue down the highway unnoticed.

"I'm getting off at the next exit," Cru said. "It's about three miles."

Red was familiar with the road. "Head west," he said. "There's a small town about five miles from here with a gas station that sells hardware and hunting supplies. It's where I buy my .22 shells."

Cru pulled into the gas station and drove around back where there were a few dumpsters and small shacks. They both got out of the car and gave it a quick inspection.

"No major damage," Cru said after checking the undercarriage.

A large German Shepherd chained to an old tire rim got up and started barking and growling. Scanning the place with shotgun in hand, Red strolled over and petted the dog, which calmed down and started wagging its tail.

"Easy, boy. Don't bite us, and I'll get you a nice hot dog," Red said. "We better get what we need and get over to the trailer. We'll have to sneak in through the back way, in case any more of these assholes are around."

Cru agreed. "Lucky all our cash and paperwork were in the trunk. Looks like we'll have to buy new furniture and clothes when we get to Albuquerque. Let's get what we need and get the hell out of here. We'll have to switch cars and trash this one before we leave the trailer."

Red went into the gas station and bought up all the ammunition available in the caliber of weapons they had, along with over the counter pain killers, bandages, bread, lunchmeat, and a hot dog. Before leaving they filled the radiator with water, and Red gave the hot dog to the German Shepherd.

They got to the trailer about three hours later, driving in on an old farming road that was seldom used. A quarter of a mile from the trailer, Red got out, took the shotgun, and ran ahead to make sure no one was waiting in ambush. Cru stood by the vehicle and kept watch.

"All clear," Red said when he returned.

They motored in, parking the car behind the trailer. The two worked fast, packing everything of importance into their other vehicle. Then they parked the bullet-riddled sedan flush to the trailer, doused everything with gasoline, and ignited it. While the trailer and car burned, Cru and red watched from a distance, sticking around long enough to make sure everything would be destroyed. Then they climbed into their remaining car and headed east.

Chapter 7

At the same time Cru and Red were retreating eastward, Alton Deem was making his escape to the south. True to his word, after three weeks and another bungled ambush, Louie Dragna put out a contract on Alton Deem. Deem and Monk were nearly killed when two of Deem's other dealers decided to cash in on Louie's lucrative offer. Barely escaping with their lives, they fled south with only the clothes on their backs and the cash in their pockets.

"I gotta take a leak," Monk whined.

Deem had no sympathy. "I told you to shut the fuck up and drive. We ain't stopping till we hit San Diego. If you had locked that door like you were supposed to, we wouldn't be in this fucking mess. Piss your pants for all I care."

Louie's men had walked into Deem's warehouse office undetected while Deem was removing cash from the safe. They didn't see Monk sitting in the corner with his .45 out. Before they could react, Monk opened fire, killing them both.

"Hey, I killed those two assholes!" Monk indignantly replied.

"After you fucking let 'em in."

"Where we goin', anyway?" Monk grumbled.

"We ain't goin' anywhere. I'm letting you off at the bus station in downtown San Diego. Then you can take the grey dog anywhere your little ass pleases."

Frowning, Monk looked over at him. "You gonna give

me my share?"

"I'm giving you what you deserve. Now shut the fuck up and keep driving."

* * *

"Deem and his whole crew are a bunch of fuckups!" Louie Dragna raged. "First he lets some amateur hustlers rip me off. Then he bungles every chance he has to take 'em out. And the assholes who work for him are incompetent morons. Where is that douche bag?"

"We think he headed south with one of his guys," one of Louie's men offered.

"Then why aren't you after them?"

The man held his hands up. "We've got every available button looking, Louie. We'll find 'em. Give us a chance already."

"I heard all that shit before! What about these fucks robbing me? They're still out there, too. Once these pricks in San Diego find out any cheap pimp that comes along can roll me over, they'll push me into the goddamn ocean!"

"Look, Louis. We think they left, too. Our man in San Bernardino told us about a fire of suspicious origin out in the desert. It burned an empty trailer and vehicle to cinders. We think it was these assholes' hideout."

"Then what are you gonna do about it?"

"We think they headed east and we got five guys on it. Three on the ground and two in the air," the man replied.

"You catch these fuckers that've turned my life to shit. You catch 'em and bring 'em to me," Louie said, jaws clenched and eyes quivering.

* * *

Traveling through the night, Red and Cru spent the next day at Joshua Tree National Park. They took shelter under a canopy of thick growth next to a large boulder on a hill, where they would be concealed yet have a commanding view of the surrounding area. .

"These dried hunting rations aren't much better than C-rats," Cru complained.

"Well, I was going to fix you a nice pan of lasagna, but I couldn't find any fresh basil."

When he first moved to California, Red was added to Aunt Tesla's list of people she spoiled with her old world recipes. He was so fond of her cooking he learned every recipe, and the smell of gourmet Italian cooking often wafted from their small apartment in LA or the trailer in the desert. People who knew them both thought it humorous that Redmond, the Native American, cooked gourmet Italian dishes for Crucianelli, the full-blooded Italian.

"Too bad. I sure could go for a nice plate of that lasagna," Cru mused. "Or how about some of your fish and rice with maple syrup?" Cru also liked the Ojibwa favorite that Red occasionally prepared.

"Well, we don't have any fish or rice or maple syrup. Other than that, we're okay. You better get used to that dehydrated beef, my friend."

"You know, Red, this place is amazing. I heard these Joshua trees are some of the oldest living things on earth."

"Yeah, it is beautiful here. I was thinking how different it is from Minnesota and Wisconsin. Beautiful in a different way. There's plenty of game here, too. We could live off the land right here. If we could stay, that is."

Both men became quiet, remembering the fix they were in.

"Yeah... if we could stay," Cru repeated quietly.

Chapter 8

Angelo Rossitello was standing next to the bar in his San Diego nightclub when Deem and Monk walked in. Deem had decided to allow Monk to stay with him, rationalizing that he might need a fall guy.

"Keep your eye on those two lowlifes," Rossitello told the floor manager. "They work for that pimp, Dragna."

Angelo Rossitello was the head of the Italian Mafia in the San Diego area, and like the Dragnas, he could see his empire eroding piece by piece from the incursions of the ever growing Mexican gangs.

The Dragnas and Rossitellos had been skirmishing off and on for several years. Greed made Rossitello bold as he attempted to expand his crime empire north in an effort to compensate for what he had been losing to the Mexican gangs. By the same token and for the same reasons, Dragna tried to gain more territory toward the south. Thus far, only a handful of people had been killed, and neither one had been able to gain a substantial foothold over the other.

Now sitting across from Deem in the musty basement of his nightclub, Rossitello narrowed his eyes. "What can I do for you?"

Taking a deep breath, Deem said, "I can help you nail Dragna." Deem sat on the edge of his seat. Two of Rossitello's men idly stood by. Monk was nowhere to be seen, not having been invited to the meeting.

Paging through a racing form, Rossitello was coy. "And assuming I was interested in nailing this Dragna fellow, how exactly would you do that, Mr. ah...Deem, is it?"

"Right, it's Deem. Alton Deem, Mr. Rossitello." Deem extended his arm in an attempt to shake hands.

Rossitello ignored the outstretched hand. "I'm listening, Deem."

Not put off by the slight, Deem continued. "Right. Well, Dragna's been getting ripped off by a couple of local yokels up in LA. They found a way to snatch a big chunk of his money and still manage to keep themselves alive."

"Old news," Rossitello stated flatly.

"Yeah, that's old news. But I know who they are," Deem said, hoping to pique Rossitello's interest.

Putting aside the racing form, Rossitello scrutinized Deem for a moment. "Okay, you got my attention. Now let's hear all of it."

* * *

After leaving the national park, Cru and Red drove to the Colorado Indian Reservation along the Colorado River near Parker, Arizona. Red knew some of the members of the four tribes from a national tribal council some years earlier. He hoped to look them up before driving on.

"You know, it's going to be around midnight when we get there," Cru said.

"Thought we could wait 'til morning to try and find them. I understand your concern—it will throw us off our schedule—but I don't want to pass up this opportunity."

"No problem, Red. We'll pick up some things during the day and then take off tomorrow night. Maybe there's a few Indian maidens around who can entertain us."

"You start sniffing around those rez girls, the local braves will make soup out of you. You better keep that thing in your pants, buddy."

"You think they'll treat your Ojibwa ass any different?" Cru wanted to know.

"Probably not, but I don't have to outrun them. All I have to do is outrun your sawed-off bow legs, and that's no problem."

"Those sawed-off bow legs moved this ass okay in Nam," Cru reminded him.

"Hell, anyone could outrun old Bin," Red said, referring to the ancient mama-san who ran a brothel in Vietnam and was an object of affection herself, on occasion.

Laughing, Cru fondly remembered Bin. "Wish old Bin was around here now."

The two slept until eight o'clock the next morning. At the rez, Red learned that all of the people he was looking for were dead: two from tuberculosis, one from alcoholism, and the other killed in Nam. Saddened, Red moped around while they resupplied at the tribal store and gas station. They purchased clothing to replace some of what was lost when their trailer was destroyed. After spending the night in the car, they departed the reservation and headed once again to Albuquerque.

The remainder of the trip was uneventful, and they reached Placitas, a suburb of Albuquerque, in good time. During the next few weeks, they rented a house and set up residency in the predominantly Mexican community.

They then initiated the process of establishing their new territory.

* * *

Angelo Rossitello sensed an opportunity. The information from Deem could tip the balance in his favor in the ongoing territory struggle with the Dragnas. Although he loathed Deem, he intended to keep him around until he could extract everything of any use.

"Put these two assholes where you can keep an eye on 'em," Rossitello told his capo who worked the harbor area of San Diego, instructing him to give Deem and Monk low-level jobs on the docks.

"Do we let 'em carry?" the capo asked.

"No. No weapons of any kind. Not even a fucking pocket knife. Let Deem have a paperwork shit job and keep that idiot Monk humping cargo. Make sure someone you trust is always with Deem, pumping him for information. When we've got everything we can out of him, he'll take a trip to the bottom of the harbor. His buddy will join him there."

Chapter 9

Once settled in Placitas, Cru sent Montrell a letter, updating him on everything that transpired since they last talked. He arranged a pay phone meeting and was now standing outside the booth in a shopping mall, waiting for the phone to ring and admiring some of the Native American jewelry on display in a nearby shop.

"You like turquoise?" the attractive shop attendant asked him.

"Is that what it is? Yeah, very pretty. Does it come out of the ground that way or do you paint it?"

"No, silly," the young woman laughed. "It comes out of the ground like that."

Cru was taken by the willowy young blond. In full hippy garb, she presented a striking figure, standing amidst the beautiful jewelry she offered.

"I'm Andrew Crucianelli, but everyone calls me Cru."

"My name's Christine. You aren't from around here, are you?"

"I'm from Arizona," he lied.

Christine was a native of the southwest and recognized Cru's accent as distinctly Midwestern. "From Arizona by way of Iowa, maybe?"

Cru changed the subject, not wanting to talk about the Midwest. "Christine's a pretty name for a pretty girl. What are you doing when you aren't peddling blue rocks?"

"I'm polishing them, Andrew. Are you hitting on me?"

"It's Cru or just Andy," Cru reminded her. "I'm in

town for a short time and don't want to have dinner alone. Join me?"

"Dinner, huh? That's pretty formal stuff for a free-spirited person, like me. Usually I eat when I'm hungry, sleep when I'm tired, and party whenever I want to."

Before Cru could reply, the phone in the booth rang. "Excuse me, that's for me. When I'm done, let me know if you're up for any of that free-spirited stuff tonight."

* * *

"So you got in a little R&R, huh? I think I'm gonna have to dock your pay," Red commented.

Cru had told Red about his trip to the mall and dinner with Christine, as well as his discussion with Montrell. "Monty's going to talk to his friend Vinnie to see if he's heard any more from his cousin in California. And of course, he keeps saying we should get out of this business completely."

"Monty always did lean to the cautious side. Not saying he's wrong, but we're kind of like halfway in and halfway out. Better to keep going forward and end it when we're ready, as opposed to trying to back out at this point, and maybe step into all kinds of shit."

"Damn, Red. You're turning into some kind of half-ass philosopher. Think I'll start calling you the Dalai Redmond."

"You better worry about what they start calling you, ace, falling in love with hippie chicks. What would Sergeant Prentice say?"

Master Sergeant Charles Prentice was their non-commissioned officer in charge, during their tour of duty in Vietnam. A wise older man, Prentice would often chide the young troops assigned to him. Anyone who particularly raised his ire would be chastised as a "damn hippie" by the grizzled old veteran.

"Yeah, old Vodka Charlie would sure as hell give me shit about it, that old coot."

"You'll probably throw away all your material goods and run off with her to some sorry commune."

"I doubt it," Cru assured. "By the way, I forgot to mention that Monty went up to see Hardy's parents a while back."

Red was glad to hear that. "Good. Hardy was his best friend and he took it pretty bad."

Red could still see Terry falling, almost in slow motion. He abruptly changed the subject. "Did you find any opportunities for us, or did you spend the whole damn day tiptoeing through the tulips with the hippies?"

"As a matter of fact, I did find an opportunity. There's a large college campus near downtown. They have an outdoor mall similar to the college I attended in the San Fernando Valley. Damn, I wish I'd been able to stay there and finish. I could have had a degree by now."

"Yeah, but I'd still be on the rez, a deadbeat drunk..."

"Well anyway, this college has the same outdoor mall setup."

"Let me guess," Red interjected.

Smiling, Cru said, "Yep, a little weasel called Banjo carries out a flourishing drug business there. Sure brings to mind our old buddy Tito. And as far as I know, there's no el jefe involved to fuck us up. Checked out a couple other leads as well, and they also appear to be small time punks working on their own. We might have stumbled into the mother lode here. What did you come up with?"

While Cru's job was to locate potential targets of opportunity, Red was tasked with learning as much as he could about any local crime syndicates or networks that might exist in the Albuquerque area. At first they thought about asking Montrell to check with Vinnie Falconnetti about it, but realized they were better off staying under the radar. Red's findings were encouraging.

"It doesn't look like the mob has any real presence here, but the Mexican gangs are flourishing. They don't seem to be as widespread or organized as the LA Mexicans, though. I didn't find any evidence of any kind of kingpin." Red paused. "One name that did keep popping up was the 'Minutemen'."

"Who the hell are the minutemen?" Cru wanted to know.

"I guess the area was infiltrated with communists trying to steal information for the Russians during the nuclear bomb testing they did out here, way back when. The Minutemen popped up to counter those efforts. They were made up of a bunch of local yokels who apparently spent more time raising hell at meetings, drinking beer, and harassing the local Mexican farm workers than chasing any commies. I guess they still have monthly meetings, but mostly to get away from their wives and get drunk—oh, and they also march in the local Fourth of July parade."

"The right wing version of the Shriners, huh?"

"I guess," Red agreed.

They spent the next few hours planning out their hit on Banjo, intending to carry it out the following weekend.

* * *

Redmond and Crucianelli were posted at their respective positions in a college mall on a Friday evening. Banjo was plying his trade nearby. The two had scouted the area three days in a row and were confident they were prepared for their mission. As usual, Cru went in while the keen-eyed Redmond kept a look out.

Circling around, Crucianelli crept up near Banjo and watched as he made a sale to two college age girls. "I can show you lovely girls around, if you need a guide," Banjo offered.

The girls politely indicated they did not require those services, paid Banjo, and left. As Banjo stood leering after them, Crucianelli moved in, pulled out his slapjack, and whacked him over the head.

"Oomph." Banjo went down like a sack of flour.

After a quick look around, Cru stepped over the unconscious man and relieved him of his money bag, drug satchel, and pistol. In some ways, they were relieved Tibbits was no longer part of their crew and had no intention of continuing his ritual of urinating on the victim.

"Let's get outta here!" Cru whispered loudly, after which he and Red made a hasty retreat to their vehicles parked in the middle of the parking lot on the opposite side of the campus. They stayed with older models, paying cash whenever they needed additional transportation.

"See you back in Placitas," Red said. He destroyed most of the drugs and took the remainder to the lair of one of Banjo's competitors, Hombre, one of the bigger dealers in the area. He scattered the drugs around the front area by the road, where anyone checking out Hombre's activities might conveniently find them. Since Red intended to call in an anonymous tip to the police, someone would conveniently find them sooner than later.

The next morning Red and Cru stashed some of the cash in a safe inside the house and deposited the remaining money in one of the safe deposit boxes they had rented.

"Not a bad take," Cru remarked.

"Good deal," Red said. "Now we can buy some furniture for this place."

"Hell, you're used to sitting on the floor in a damn teepee anyway. Why waste money on furniture?"

"Teepee, my ass. You just want to throw all that money away on that hippie chick you're sweet on."

It was true. Cru was seeing Christine on a daily basis. When they weren't attending rock concerts, they were hiking in the desert or just hanging out somewhere. Cru seemed to be happy, and Red was glad for him. Things were going very well in their new location.

The next weekend they planned to knock over a dealer at McDuffie Park. The dealer was referred to as El Cato. As usual, they scouted the area thoroughly for three days.

As a means of staying sharp, Red and Cru routinely

traded duties. They knew from their military training that this kept them both focused on all aspects of the operation. Tonight, Red would make the hit, while Cru would perform lookout and evasive tactics afterwards.

El Cato was standing near a large tree, in between a closed concession stand and public restroom facilities. Red watched Cato make several sales. During a lull in sales, Cato bent his head to light a cigarette. Before he finished, Red eased up behind him and knocked him out cold with his slapjack. El Cato's head hit the corner of a curb on the way down and he suffered a nasty gash. Red checked the man's head, relieved him of his money and drugs, made sure he was breathing, and left.

Cru took the drugs, planted them by another dealer's home base, phoned in a tip to the police, and met Red back in Placitas. He sensed Red was uneasy.

"Everything okay, buddy?"

"The dude's head smacked the curb on the way down. He seemed all right, but it could have been more serious."

Cru understood Red's sensitivities. Even in Nam, when forced to kill, he expressed compassion for his victims.

"These men have chosen a dangerous profession, Red."

"So have we, my friend, so have we," Red replied soberly.

Chapter 10

On a pleasant Friday evening in Long Beach, one of Louie Dragna's drug peddlers, known as Quinn, was enjoying a brisk business at the Long Beach City College. He was positioned outside the auditorium where a rock concert had just let out.

Having fired Alton Deem and targeted him for death, Louie assumed the day to day management of all of Deem's operations. He ruled with an iron fist, and let everyone know that if they found Deem or any of the perps who were robbing his drug dealers, he would personally handle their punishment.

As Quinn was about to wrap up for the night, a man in camouflage approached from behind. Hearing the man approach, Quinn turned and said, "What the fuck you want, asshole?"

Before Quinn could make another move, the man pulled out a slapjack and rendered him unconscious.

"I'll show you what I want, you piece of shit." The man relieved Quinn of his money, along with his .45 caliber pistol and the remaining drugs. Before leaving, he urinated on Quinn's prone body.

* * *

Louie Dragna was in a rage. "These fuckers are at it again? While these cocksuckers are robbing me blind, you worthless shits are running around blowing my money. That asshole Deem has to be behind this!"

Only one of Dragna's subordinate's dared speak up. "We've searched high and low for these guys, Mr. Dragna.

I can assure you we're doing the best we can."

This further enraged Dragna, who picked up his coffee cup and threw it. Although the man ducked, he and the men on both sides of him were sprayed with the contents of the cup.

"Find these assholes, you fucking louses. Now get out of my sight."

* * *

Doug Montrell was surprised to find a note in his door from his friend Vinnie Falconnetti. He called Vinnie from the same pay phone he used when calling Cru and Red. "What's up, Vinnie?"

"My cousin in LA tells me your friends have been busy again."

Not wanting to tip Vinnie off that the two had moved out of the area, Montrell said, "Haven't spoken with them in a while, Vinnie. What's going on?"

"Seems they've hit several more of Dragna's operations. They're seriously lightening his cash reserves, and my old buddy Louie is fucking pissed."

"I'm under the impression that my friends are only involved in the import export business, Vinnie."

"Whatever you say, Doug. But I'm kind of surprised they've taken it to this level. Robbing drug dealers is one thing; murder is another."

* * *

"Fuck, we've been set up." Crucianelli had received the news about the Los Angeles drug dealer robberies from Montrell during their long-distance phone call. "It seems someone is copycatting us in LA, only now they've raised the stakes considerably. Five drug dealers have been hit, mimicking our methods even down to Tibbits's lame 'signature' of pissing on the fuckers. But the last one they hit, they bashed his head in hard enough to kill him. The bastard still pissed on him, anyway."

Red took a moment to digest the information. "Gotta be Deem. He's filling his pockets and setting us up." But Red wasn't completely sure. "Except I didn't think Deem had the brains or the balls to pull off something like this."

Crucianelli agreed. "It does seem out of character. Montrell says Vinnie promised he won't reveal his knowledge about our previous involvement, but that could change based on circumstances. He also says Vinnie thinks someone big is involved, someone who has his sights on the Dragna empire."

"Dragna hasn't exerted the energy to find us since we moved out here and left him alone, but I'm thinking that's gonna change now," Red said. "I think we better hide another trailer out in the boonies, just in case this place gets sniffed out. And maybe we should lay low for a while."

"Yeah. We'll have to do a better job of concealing our presence than we did in California. If Montrell's buddy can track us down, so can Dragna. Maybe we should have assumed false identities when we got here."

"Well, other than Falconnetti ferreting out my name from the warehouse agreement, nothing else has come back to bite us," Cru said.

"We've been lucky...so far."

* * *

Angelo Rossitello was in a good spirits. His plan to cut into the Dragna operations undetected was working well. No doubt Louie Dragna was suspicious of his powerful rival to the south, but as yet he had no way of connecting him to the problems he was now experiencing. The only possible way Dragna could tie Rossitello to the attacks on his organization would be for him to obtain the knowledge that Deem and Monk were now in the employ of Angelo Rossitello. Their status, however, would soon be irreversibly changed.

PART TWO

*"What should I have known or written
had I been a quiet, mercantile politician or
a lord in waiting?
A man must travel and turmoil,
or there is no existence."*

~Lord Byron

Chapter 11

L ieutenant George Dooley had been assigned to the Los Angeles County organized crime unit for several years. He worked his way up through the ranks, after serving four years with the United States Air Force in security police. In early 1971, Dooley found himself investigating what appeared to be a turf war among some of the remaining Anglo drug dealers in the Los Angeles area. Two bodies had surfaced thus far. Dooley was now at the morgue with the medical examiner.

"Anything on the body that was in the water?"

"No," the medical examiner said. "If the perps hadn't blown his head off, we could have run x-rays."

"What's next?" Dooley asked.

"The guy has some unusual trauma to his buttocks. They may be from some type of special immunization injection. I intend to check that out."

This piqued Dooley's curiosity. "May I see it?"

The examiner nodded and handed Dooley a tube of Vicks Vaporub. "Put some of this under your nose. The smell won't be pretty."

The two went into the morgue, and the examiner pulled out one of the refrigerated drawers. The body was grossly swollen, and there were numerous bullet holes in the torso and what remained of the head. He carefully turned the body so Dooley could have a look at the trauma on the man's buttocks.

Noting Dooley's demeanor the examiner said, "You recognize that type of deformity?"

"Yes, it appears to be the hump from a G&G shot. Do me a favor. Run five copies of the forensic report and have them sent to my office as soon as possible."

The next morning, the reports from the medical examiner were on his desk. The information contained the man's height, weight, and approximate age. It also included information about the man's ethnic background. Dooley reviewed the report with his assistant, Sergeant Richard Martin.

"Do a missing persons check for any Caucasian males who have served in the military in the last three years," Dooley told his assistant.

"You think the dude's a GI, Skip?" the assistant asked.

"Ex-GI, maybe. Young men don't usually get gamma globulin injections unless they're required. The only people I know of who routinely get them are men pulling duty in Vietnam or some other third world hellhole. Let's see what we come up with."

"You think it's the same bunch that whacked Quinn?"

Dooley had given that some thought as well. "Same MO. It's curious, though. For some reason these guys have taken it up a couple notches. Before they started killing these assholes, they seemed happy just robbing them."

"Maybe they're getting pragmatic, Skip. Dead men don't tell stories, seek revenge, or compete for business."

"Could be," Dooley said, "could be."

* * *

Lieutenant Dooley and the organized crime unit were not the only ones paying attention to the drug dealer conflict occurring in their territory.

Rafael Tijenera was sitting in his garage in Santa Ana listening to one of his subordinates. Rafael was the head of one of the large Mexican gangs that were gradually taking over Southern California.

"I think it is the Chipileño. They chase Deem away and take his territory. We should kill the jefe, Louie Dragna," the man said. Mexicans commonly referred to Italians as Chipileño, an area in Mexico where many had migrated upon leaving Italy.

Rafael looked at the man derisively. "That's easy for you to say. You only have your little whore and the shirt on your back to worry about. The Chipileño are protected by the police and the judges they have in their pockets. A war with them brings us much trouble. That will change one day, but until then we must be smart in what we do."

"But we must do something, el jefe."

"Our spy thinks he knows these men, and he is watching them. They are stealing from each other and now killing each other. Already our business has increased because of this. So long as things remain as they are, we have no problem. When that changes, we'll take care of it," Rafael told him.

Chapter 12

Andrew Crucianelli was feeling good. He and Christine had taken in a rock concert by the group War the previous evening, then gone back to her place and partied. Cru left her house and headed for Placitas around three in the morning. Still a little high, he wasn't totally alert or he might have noticed the bread truck following him.

"The Cisco Kid was a friend of mine," Cru sang, while keeping the beat by tapping the steering wheel. The bread truck was now directly to his right on the four-lane street. As the driver sped up to match Cru's speed, a shotgun slid out the window directly behind the driver. At the exact moment the man fired, Cru, applied the brakes, intending to make a left turn at the intersection. The blast of the shotgun jolted Cru out of his complacency, and although the deadly shot missed him, it shattered his windshield, spraying him with glass.

"Fuck!" Cru screamed as he wrenched the wheel left, causing his vehicle to spin around and slide. The momentum of the bread truck kept it hurtling down the road. The driver of the bread van skidded into a U-turn and sped back at full throttle toward Cru's still sliding car. Having regained his wits, Cru helplessly watched the oncoming truck in horror. With his vehicle finally slowed enough to gain control, he wrenched the wheel to the right and floored the accelerator, moving away from the speeding truck. The heavy bread truck rammed the rear of his car, threatening to send it spinning again.

The shooter shouted at the driver. "Get alongside of him. I don't have a shot."

"I'm trying!" the driver yelled as he attempted to maneuver the truck into a better position.

Having none of that, Cru swerved from side to side, preventing the truck from advancing into position. Cru's lighter vehicle pulled away and sped out of range. After two more blocks, he made a fast turn down a one-way street, going the wrong way. The bread truck was unable to make the turn, but slowed down and executed a quick U-turn, taking up the chase again.

"Fuck!" Cru screamed again as a semitrailer delivery truck appeared, heading straight for him. The semi driver leaned on his air horn as Cru jumped the curb and drove down the sidewalk, sideswiping the passing truck. The screeching of metal on metal was soon drowned out by the head-on collision of the semi with the bread van, which could neither get out of the way nor stop. The collision squeezed the semi further into Cru's vehicle, and all three vehicles came to a halt. Cru grabbed his .38 Smith & Wesson, jumped out of the car, and took cover behind it. When nothing moved for a minute, he eased forward to the front of the two trucks.

The semi driver was moaning—shook up, but not seriously hurt.

After ensuring that the semi driver was in no immediate danger, Cru crept into position near the bread truck. He saw the driver hanging halfway out of the windshield with part of the broken steering wheel protruding from his neck. The shooter, eyes glazed and tongue protruding, was pressed against the driver's seat by a large cabinet that had crushed him on impact. Cru moved back to his car and removed everything of importance. With no witnesses in sight, he took off down the alley. When he'd put enough distance between himself and the bread truck, Cru called Red from a pay phone and hid until Red could pick him up.

"You look like you've been run over by a truck," Red said.

"Damn close, Red, damn close." Cru was cut up and bruised a bit, but suffered no major injuries.

"Drink this," Red advised when they got back to the house, handing Cru a shot of Wild Turkey.

Cru downed it quickly and sat quietly for a time.

"Looks like they found us, buddy." Red said.

"Yeah, but who is 'they'? I've thought about it all the way back. It just doesn't seem right for the local talent to have caught up with us already."

"Deem," Red muttered.

"Deem or some other asshole from LA."

"I sure don't feel like moving again," Red said.

"I don't either. Let's hole up for a while. I think we should go ahead and get that trailer we looked at."

Cru and Red had found several trailers that would suit their needs. Two of them were already on land they could lease. One of them, being very secluded, lent itself to their needs very well. They signed an agreement and drove out under cover of darkness the next night. They had equipment and supplies in their Placitas garage, so no additional shopping trips were necessary.

"Looks like we'll be living on jackrabbit stew again," Cru commented first thing the next morning.

"Yep, might even snag some roadrunners and rattlers for extra flavor."

Cru laughed. "You can keep your damn rattlers. And if Wily Fucking Coyote can't catch a roadrunner, how do you figure on doing it?"

"Hell, I can shoot better than that mange-infested coyote. And rattler is pretty damn good. Probably no worse than that mystery meat they used to put in those C-rations."

"Big difference: we didn't know what that shit was. We could pretend it was good," Cru protested.

The new hide-away in the desert was exactly what Red

and Cru needed. It was high enough to afford them a view of anything coming along the road that wound through the desert, yet hidden in thick vegetation so as to conceal it from passing traffic. Like their California hideout, there was an old back road which allowed them an alternate entrance or exit, if need be. After staying three days, they figured it might be time to head back to Albuquerque to do some investigating.

They were on the old porch, sipping tequila and enjoying the sunset when Cru said, "I could just stay right here."

"Would be nice," Red agreed, and then added, "We have to talk about something, buddy."

Cru tensed up a bit. "Yeah?"

"How well do you know Christine?"

Before Cru could protest, Red held up his hand. "I know she treats you right and you think a lot of her. I'm not saying she's responsible, but could someone who knows her be the one that tried to whack you?"

Cru thought it over. "I could never believe Christine would be involved with those pukes, but to be honest, I have had thoughts about some of the people she hangs with. There's a real collection of humanity in that tie-dyed address book of hers. Most of them are harmless hippies who use a little pot, speed, and acid."

"Most of them? What about the rest of them?"

With his hands out, Cru shrugged his shoulders and slowly shook his head.

Chapter 13

The investigation Lieutenant Dooley ordered turned up several cases of recently discharged military personnel who were on the missing persons list. Of those, five were Caucasian. And of those five, three were Vietnam veterans who had either taken their own life or died from a drug overdose.

"Damn shame what's happening to our returning veterans these days," said Dooley to his assistant. "I hear way too much of this shit. What about the other two?"

"One was a sailor stationed at Subic Bay. He had a girlfriend over there, and his brother thinks he went back to find her."

"Uh huh, and what about the other one?"

"That one's kind of interesting, Skip. Ex-army, last duty station Vietnam."

Noting the look on his assistant's face, Dooley prodded "And?"

"I called his parents; the guy's originally from Anaheim. His old man answered the phone. Evidently he didn't get along with the kid too well. Said as far as he was concerned, the drug dealing bastard could stay lost."

"You don't say," Dooley commented. "See if you can get hold of his mother. Maybe she'll talk to us. What's the guy's name anyway?"

"Tibbits. Robert Tibbits."

* * *

Crucianelli was sitting comfortably in a bean bag chair in Christine's small bungalow. The pungent aroma of burning Thai stick and patchouli oil permeated the air.

"I missed you," Christine said.

"Yeah, sorry about not calling for a couple days. Red and I were out hunting and there were no phones anywhere to be found," Cru lied.

"I didn't realize you guys were going on a hunting trip. You never mentioned it."

"Sorry about that, too. We were out tooling around and Red, well you know Red, that damn Injun just up and decided we needed to go hunting." Cru hoped Christine would buy the story.

"Didn't think elk were in season yet." Christine hadn't always been an urban hippie. She was raised in the foothills in the nearby desert, and her father and both brothers were avid outdoorsmen.

"No, we were after jackrabbits. Red just can't pass up an opportunity to shoot at those quick little buggers."

"Well goodness, Cru, judging from the shape you're in, those rabbits must have been some tough little buggers." Christine couldn't help but notice all the bruises on his body when they made love after Cru first arrived.

Brushing that aside with a gesture, Cru thought it was time to get down to business. "Christine, how well do you know Teo and Drummond?"

Teo and Drummond were the two men Christine routinely purchased marijuana from. They were also part of the large group of diverse people she partied with on occasion. Cru had reason to be suspicious of them, as they were both shady characters involved with local drug gangs. At previous gatherings at Christine's when the two were present, Cru had gotten the feeling they were watching him.

"How do you mean?" Chris became somewhat defensive. "They're different. Lots of my friends are different. I try not to judge people."

Cru sensed Christine's discomfort and decided not to pursue it. "Sorry, just curious I guess. Couple of my tapes were missing from my car after the last party over here."

"So you decided my friends are thieves." Christine was now irritated.

"Sorry, I'm just pissed and a little paranoid, I guess. Forget I brought it up."

* * *

"Is every asshole that works for me incompetent?" Louie Dragna fumed.

"Sorry, Chief. We thought we had 'em nailed, but the bastards slipped away. Just blind fucking luck."

"Blind fucking luck, my ass. You dipshits couldn't catch a cold at Christmas time. This is the bunch that's been robbing me blind for six months. We get a fucking good lead that they're setting up out in Bubba land. We isolate them. And you assholes fuck it up. Again."

The man hoped to placate Dragna. "It probably ain't even the same bunch, Chief."

With murderous eyes, Dragna looked at the man. "You better tell me when you intend to find out."

Chapter 14

Lieutenant Dooley and Sergeant Martin received permission from Robert Tibbits's mother to visit her and conduct an interview.

"I know this is a bad time for you, Mrs. Tibbits. I am very sorry about the death of your son. How are you doing?"

"Thank you for your concern, Lieutenant Dooley. I'm managing...barely. What information can I help you with?"

"For the past several months, a small group of men have been robbing drug dealers in the LA area. Word has it that these men are a group of military veterans, recently back from Southeast Asia."

"Drug dealers fight with each other all the time, don't they, Lieutenant?" Mrs. Tibbits asked.

"They do, ma'am, but the men perpetrating these robberies aren't drug dealers. They rob the dealers for the money and throw the drugs away."

"It seems to me that a drug dealer being robbed is poetic justice, Lieutenant."

"I don't disagree with you, Mrs. Tibbits. Unfortunately the robberies have now escalated into murder," Dooley said.

"And...you believe my Robert was a drug dealer... murdered by these people?"

Lieutenant Dooley was shaking his head. "No, ma'am, we think Robert may have been involved with the men robbing the drug dealers and destroying the drugs. We believe the drug dealers caught him and killed him."

Mrs. Tibbits absorbed this information with a look of despair on her face and began sobbing. Striving to bring her tears under control, she stammered, "When Bobby... returned from Vietnam...he was changed. The young happy boy who went over there...one year earlier ... came back a much different person." She covered her face with her hands and continued to sob.

Dooley waited a few moments and gently handed her a tissue. "Can you continue, ma'am?"

Nodding, she went on, "Bobby didn't seem to be well. He...he had this depression...and anger in him. He wasn't interested in his old friends at all and didn't have too much use for his family, either, for that matter. His father heard that Bobby got into some kind of trouble smuggling drugs out of Vietnam, and after that they had a very bad relationship. Bobby moved out after two weeks, and we weren't sure where he went."

"Did he ever contact you?"

"Yes, he called in the mornings sometimes, when he knew his father was at work. At first he seemed unhappy, but then after a few weeks his mood seemed to pick up. And then he started sending me money. I just assumed he got a job and was back to his old self."

"How much money did he send you, Mrs. Tibbits?" Dooley's assistant asked.

Looking around the room, Mrs. Tibbits quietly told him, "A lot. Robert sent me a lot of money."

* * *

Cru and Red determined that no one had traced them to their Placitas location and were discussing Christine's two friends, Teo and Drummond.

"I'll check them out myself," Crucianelli said. "They always work together, so whatever comes up for one will apply to both of them."

"Sounds dangerous, buddy. I don't think you should handle this alone."

"I'll stay as far away as necessary, strictly reconnaissance. Mostly, we need to find out who they hang with and who they correspond with."

"Take the Green Burrito," Red said, referring to the used Chevy van they purchased from a hippie who needed money. The exterior was lime green decorated with colored flower decals. The interior included dark paneling, shag carpeting, and tinted glass. Such vans could be found all over the Southwestern United States in the late 1960's and early 1970's, so the vivid colors and decorations, though gaudy, were inconspicuous. As a bonus, the van was tricked out with a 396-cubic-inch engine with a four-barrel carburetor.

After loading everything they needed for a three-day trip, Cru called Christine and told her he'd be out hunting rabbits for a few days.

"I think she's getting suspicious. Not sure if she thinks I got another babe hidden away somewhere or if I'm some kind of narc."

"I can take over for a while, buddy. She'll forget about you in no time," Red commented.

"Yeah, you'd introduce her to your 'peace pipe,' huh?"

"Damn straight."

Cru nodded. "Might be a good idea. Then she'd realize how good she has it with me."

* * *

Monk thought Angelo Rossitello was an okay dude. The dock job Rossitello gave Monk provided him with a decent income, allowing him to support his rather hefty amphetamine habit. It also gave him ample opportunity to steal anything he could get his hands on. He was about halfway through his shift when his supervisor came to see him.

"I need you on another job that's shorthanded. Follow me."

Monk followed his supervisor along the pier for about ten minutes until they arrived at a small fenced in area where the International Longshoremen conducted union business.

"What we gotta do here?" Monk was curious.

"These boxes just came in from Japan. They're full of stereo equipment. We're gonna take our share before we send them on. You don't have a problem with that, do you?"

"Hell, no, boss. I don't give a fuck."

"We all help ourselves to some of this shit, right?"

Not realizing he was being baited, Monk incriminated himself. "I sure do. Got myself a nice silk suit just the other night."

With an evil smile, Monk's supervisor revealed a grappling hook he'd been concealing in his right hand. "That's nice, 'cause that's the last fucking thing you'll ever boost, asshole."

With a look of terror Monk turned to run, but a burly man appeared directly in front of him and grabbed him by the throat with one huge hand.

"Where you think you're going, punk?"

Monk struggled helplessly as the man turned him around to face the supervisor, who gored him in the scrotum with the large grappling hook. Thrashing wildly and in horrible pain, Monk was unable to scream, as the burly man clasped his hand firmly over Monk's mouth. The supervisor then jerked the grappling hook all the way up into Monk's abdomen, completely disemboweling him.

"Put him in the crate and seal it."

The burly man carried Monk's now lifeless body to a nearby crate, put it in, and gathered up the intestines which had been dragging along, pushing them inside the crate with Monk's body. He then placed the lid on the crate, and nailed it shut.

Chapter 15

Lieutenant Dooley learned that Robert Tibbits's last known address was Van Nuys, California, and that he'd been attending the community college nearby. His assistant Sergeant Martin arranged a meeting with the dean of students.

"What kind of student was Mr. Tibbits?" Dooley asked Ms. Stovern, the acting dean.

"He was an average student, academically. And since he served in the military, he was a bit older and more mature than most of the other students here. But it's not like they looked up to him. If anything, they seemed to avoid him."

"Was he involved in any extracurricular activities?" Dooley's assistant asked.

"I believe he was involved with the campus veterans group. With all the men returning from the war, the group has grown considerably in size and scope."

"Can you give us a contact for that group?" Dooley asked.

"Sure, I have a copy of their organization's information right here." Ms. Stovern fumbled through one of her drawer files and retrieved a sheet of paper from a folder. "The group has a new president. Here's his number."

"We'll give him a call. Thank you for your help, ma'am." Dooley said.

* * *

Crucianelli hid behind a garbage dumpster in an alley next to a warehouse in downtown Albuquerque. He had tailed Teo and Drummond all the way from Christine's house in an effort to find out if they were responsible for the attack on him. Cru had been watching Christine's house for half a day when the two showed up, stayed for a short time and drove to the warehouse.

After fifteen minutes, Cru crept up to the warehouse and stopped next to a grimy window where an inside light was shining through. He had an M-16 with him, one of the two Tibbits had given Cru and Red from his stash of smuggled weapons from Vietnam. Making sure he was locked and loaded, Cru listened closely to the conversation through the slightly open window.

"Like to bang that bitch, huh?" someone was asking.

"You wouldn't?"

"You know I would. Too bad she's hung up on that fucking GI. She won't give me his name, says it's confidential. Anyway, if those two assholes weren't such fuck-ups, he'd be out of the picture by now."

"Ex-GI, and hey, they almost got him. The bastard's just fucking lucky."

"Almost, my ass. You can bullshit me all you want, but the man in LA don't care about your sorry excuses. He'll cut your legs off and pack your ass in concrete. When do you plan on taking care of this shit?"

"We may not have got him, but we got his vehicle. We'll run him down."

This did not concern Cru since he and Red had started sanitizing their vehicles, ensuring there was nothing to trace back to them. It was a laborious process, involving removing the VIN numbers, laundering the bills of sales, obtaining false plates, and most importantly, leaving no personal effects anywhere in the vehicle. No, anyone attempting to run an ID off any of their vehicles would experience a fruitless pursuit. Cru was surprised that these men had not attempted to coerce Christine for the information. He suspected that would change soon.

Peeking through the crack in the window opening, Cru could see into the small warehouse office. Teo and Drummond stood near a large Hispanic man and a redheaded man with a pockmarked face. The redhead seemed to be doing all the talking.

As Cru started to creep away, the redhead spoke again. "Well, what about that bitch? You think she tipped him off?"

Cru stopped dead in his tracks and listened.

"Not to worry," Teo said. "That poor hippie chick doesn't know it, but she is about to have an overdose."

Alarmed, Cru turned back and, after checking through the window again, walked over to the metal door leading into the office. He slowly turned the doorknob and eased the door open until he had a clear view of the entire office.

"Motherfucker!" Drummond shouted, alerting the other men to the intruder.

Pop...pop...pop. Cru squeezed off three rounds quick as he could, putting one round through Drummond's head, one round through Teo's head and one round into the chest of the pockmarked redheaded man.

Drummond's head exploded like a watermelon, splattering blood, brains, and skull matter all over the office, including its remaining occupants. His body now sat frozen in its chair, arms slack.

The bullet that hit Teo caught him directly in the right eye and exited through the rear of his skull, spraying the file cabinets behind him with bloody debris. His lifeless body slumped down over a garbage can.

The redhead sat clasping his chest, rasping and gasping for air. An unpleasant odor filled the room as his body voided itself of all waste before he, too, expired.

"Chingada madre!" the large Mexican yelled. Grazed in the shoulder by the round that went through Teo's head, he lunged toward the door like a bull, crashing into Cru and sending him sprawling. As the man's momentum carried him completely through the door and into an adjacent metal wall, he yelled, "Son of the bitch," this time in fractured English. He bounced off the metal siding and landed on his back like an upended turtle, temporarily stunned.

Recovering quickly, Crucianelli ran up to him and pointed the muzzle of his M-16 directly at his face.

"No disparar, no disparar, no shoot me," the prone man pleaded.

Breathing heavily, Cru kept the muzzle pointed at the man's head. "Stay the fuck down, asshole, or I'll shoot your ass right now."

Watching the man intently, Cru stepped back to the office door and policed his spent shells.

"Get your ass up and get moving." Cru gestured several times until the man, now understanding, got up and walked slowly in front of Cru until they reached the vehicle. Holding the rifle on the man, Cru ordered him inside the back of the van, where he handcuffed his wrist to a floor gusset. He then got out a roll of duct tape and taped the man's mouth. Swigging a large gulp from a bottle of Tequila, Cru rested for a minute to steady his nerves. The adrenaline of his recent combat slowly subsided, and he started the van. The Mexican started grunting loudly through his gag. From his facial expressions, Cru realized the man wanted a slug of the Tequila. Cru couldn't help but laugh at that. "No comprendo, amigo."

* * *

The screams coming from Mario Dragna's lavish Bel Air home pierced the air. A large container had been dropped off at the front gate and then moved to the foyer by an onsite handyman. Mario's wife was expecting a shipment of china from the northern region of Manchuria, which she intended to display with the rest of her valuable collection. But the crate had been delivered on its side and she was fearful the china was ruined. Minutes before she'd watched nervously as the handyman pried the lid off the shipping crate side panel. She couldn't seem to stop screaming after the swollen, mutilated body of Monk—along with most of his intestines—fell out of the large wooden container onto her shiny ceramic tile.

Chapter 16

Once she regained her composure, Mario Dragna's wife called the police to report the contents of the dreadful package that had been delivered to her home. Since Dragna was one of the names on the Los Angeles organized crime unit's list, the call came to Dooley's attention.

The body was not hard to identify, as Monk had his full name obligingly tattooed across his back.

"Think it was the Mexicans?" Lieutenant Dooley's assistant asked.

Dooley wasn't sure. "Could be anyone: Rossitello, the Mexicans, or the Crew for that matter." The latter referred to the casual name being applied to Crucianelli, Redmond, and the now deceased Tibbits.

"Monk's not exactly one of our high end slime balls, Skip."

"Exactly. He wasn't even considered a standing member of a street gang, as far as I recall," said Dooley. "But we do know he hooked up with Alton Deem on occasion. Hard to say who whacked him or why. I'm not even sure if they sent the body to Mario by mistake or intentionally. Louie Dragna most certainly would have swept it under the rug until he could take revenge. Sending it to Mario's delicate little wife raised a thousand dollars' worth of hell."

"And as you suspected, no prints or anything of use on the container," the sergeant reported.

"Send this thing to the morgue. We're going to pay a visit to Louie Dragna," Dooley told him.

* * *

Crucianelli backed the van all the way into the garage and closed the garage door before getting Red. He then opened the back cargo doors, displaying his tethered captive.

"Who the hell is this?" Redmond wanted to know.

"Don't know his name yet. He was with those two assholes, Teo and Drummond, along with some redheaded motherfucker. They did indeed put those two men up to the attempt on my life. And they were also planning to kill Christine."

"What happened to the others?"

"I don't know what came over me, Red. When I heard them laughing about killing Christine, I just went berserk and ran into the warehouse. Before I knew what was happening, I had wasted them with the 16. This guy's got a scratch on his shoulder from one of the rounds. I'm guessing it's hurting pretty good right about now."

"Damn!" was all Red could say. He ripped the gag from the captive's mouth.

Though semiconscious, the Mexican started moaning, "Agua...Agua, por favor."

"Let me get this prick some water. I'm going to keep the bastard alive until I can pump him for all he's got," Cru said.

Red didn't say anything right away. If Cru felt the man needed killing, he would not interfere, but he did have concerns.

"Maybe we should just drive him out to the Sandia and get it done now if you think he needs to be killed, before anyone gets wind of him around here."

"Good thought. I'll pack up and get him out there right away. You coming?"

"Yeah, I want to hear what he's got to say," Red replied.

* * *

"You fucking bring this shit into my home? My home?" Mario Dragna was in a rage. "My wife hasn't slept for three days. And the fucking neighbors are all giving me the stink eye."

"What the fuck you blame me for?" Louie countered. "I didn't kill the little asshole, and I damn sure didn't ship his sorry carcass to Cinderella's castle."

"Don't you bad-mouth my wife. And you sure as hell are responsible. That little piss-ant worked for you, and whoever did this is sending you a message. They knew they'd get more mileage out of it by sending his sorry dead ass to my place. Because you're a psychopathic killer and wouldn't give a shit one way or the other."

With a murderous look, Louie Dragna became very quiet. Then he said, "All these years I've done the hard work. Yeah, the dirty work. But half the dirty money from all that work is sitting in bank accounts under your name." Louie jabbed his finger in the air. "You never turned any of it down, but you and your wife fly around like a couple of stravagante. You go to your fucking tea parties and your opera and all your put-on bullshit and pretend you don't know where the money comes from. Fuck you!"

Mario Dragna looked down at the floor, back at Louie, and shook his head.

"I sure miss Dario," he eventually said.

Now Louie felt bad and a few minutes passed in silence. "Didn't mean to let you have it like that, brother. I miss Dario, too."

Dario Dragna was Mario's twin, and they were close; as close as only twins can get. Dario never followed in their father's footsteps like Mario and Louie. He was an eagle scout and a brilliant student with both scholastic and athletic scholarships to college, the all-American boy.

When the American public first started hearing about Vietnam in the early sixties, the strange little nation in Southeast Asia was not even a thought in Dario's head. But soon after college, as he had always done, Dario chose a difficult path. He became a pilot in the Air Force. Dario was sent to Vietnam in 1962, flying reconnaissance missions.

The O2-A Dario was flying disappeared somewhere near the Cambodian border, and Dario was never heard from again. Their parents never recovered from the loss, both going to their graves heartbroken.

Now remembering the good times with their brother, both men settled down and quietly embraced. Softly, Louie said, "We'll be okay, Mario. Tell your wife I'm sorry this happened. I'll make it up to you both."

Chapter 17

Louie Dragna agreed to meet with Lieutenant Dooley and his sergeant at the Teamster's Hall in El Monte. Dragna had been the head of the union for years, if in name only.

"How do you take your coffee, gentlemen?" he asked.

"Just black for me," Dooley said.

"None for me. I'm fine," his assistant said.

Dooley got to the point. "Mr. Dragna, the mutilated man that your sister-in-law was unfortunate enough to receive in her home was a known associate of Alton Deem."

Dragna moved his hand in a sweeping gesture. "So?"

"So, Mr. Dragna, Alton Deem was known to have been under your employ for several years."

"I have many people in my employ, Lieutenant. I can hardly be expected to keep track of them all. I have interests in many different businesses and each one has several layers of management. People come and go all the time."

Dooley leaned forward and handed Dragna a photo. The photo was one of Louie and Alton Deem entering a warehouse. "You recognize that man, Mr. Dragna?"

"Can't say I do, Lieutenant."

"That's Alton Deem, Mr. Dragna."

"Just happened to be entering the building the same time I was. What are you getting at?"

Dooley handed Dragna five more photos. Each one was of Louie and Alton entering the same warehouse on different dates. "Hard to believe these are all coincidental."

Studying the photos, Dragna appeared to suddenly

recognize Deem. "Wait a minute. Now I recall who that is. He worked security in one of my warehouses. Anyone buzzed in gets escorted in and out. Standard procedure, Lieutenant."

Frowning, Dooley saw that Dragna was stonewalling. "Rather odd that the same man would be the escort on so many different occasions, especially considering that some of these were taken early in the morning, while others were snapped at night."

"Probably changed shifts. That's a common occurrence with many security firms who require their employees to frequently change shifts. Discourages corruption from creeping in," Dragna said. "They like to shake things up."

Dooley's assistant was getting impatient. "You're a slippery one, aren't you, Dragna."

This was the opening Dragna had been waiting for. "Lieutenant, I agreed to meet with you in good faith. Since Sergeant Martin, your assistant, has found it necessary to insult me, I must now put an end to this meeting."

Frustrated, but with no other recourse, Dooley stood up to leave. "If you happen to recall any details about Alton Deem, be sure to contact me."

Back in the car, Dooley's assistant said, "Sorry, Skip. I just couldn't stand there and listen to that guy's bullshit any longer."

"Hey, you made a mistake. We all do," said Dooley. But he had an uneasy feeling about the incident.

* * *

Red, Cru, and their captive arrived at the trailer in the middle of the night, bringing enough supplies for an extended stay. They put the Mexican in an old chicken coop which was heavily reinforced to keep out coyotes and bobcats. They handcuffed him to a wall stud, left him some bread and water, and padlocked the door. Early the next morning, they returned to confront the man.

"Place stinks," Cru commented upon entering.

"Asshole shit his pants," Red said. He picked up a hose that ran from the house and doused the man thoroughly. The Mexican sputtered and coughed, but otherwise took it stoically.

"Kill me now," he said in heavily accented, but understandable, English.

"Well, good. You know English, so we won't have to get an interpreter to squeeze all the shit out of your sorry ass," Cru said.

"Si, I know English," the man muttered.

"Who's the patrón from California?" Cru demanded.

"I not know."

"Who the fuck in California set you assholes on me?" Cru asked loudly.

"I not know, Señor," the man repeated.

Looking around, Cru picked up the hose and hosed the Mexican for several minutes until the man started to turn blue.

"Who's in California?" Cru said, even louder. He temporarily directed the hose away from the man.

Raising his unfettered arm, the man said, "Stop, por favor, stop."

Cru put the hose back on the man.

"Okay. Okay. I tell you now. Stop, por favor, stop!"

Cru turned the hose off at the nozzle and waited.

Resigned to die, but not willing to withstand another cold dousing, the man croaked, "His name Dragna."

* * *

"This fucking cop is getting to be a real pain in the ass," Louie Dragna complained. Lieutenant Dooley had called him again, the day after the interview at the teamster's hall.

"Why isn't he out chasing the fucking Mexicans? Those assholes kill more people in one week than we do in a year," said the man with Louie.

"That shit don't count," Dragna said, highly indignant. "You can kill all the spics and niggers you want, but let one worthless, drug-snorting white moron like that asshole Monk get his stupid ass killed, and the fucking cops act like you assassinated the pope."

"You gonna call downtown?" the associate asked.

"You're damn right. All those old bastards have been feeding from the Dragna trough for a long time. They can get off their fat asses and earn it for a change."

"No word on Deem yet, either?"

"No...but I wish it had been that jag-off that spilled out of the fucking crate," Dragna mused. "It would have made all this bullshit worthwhile. The more I think about it, the more I'm thinking that prick in San Diego is responsible."

"Fat Angelo, you mean?" Dragna's associate said slowly.

"That fucker can't take me out himself. He's gotta set me up to do it," Dragna seethed.

"When we gonna start pushing back, Chief?"

Louie frowned. "I'll have to wait until the heat is off. Meanwhile, Rossitello controls all the longshoremen in San Diego. I think it's time they had some union problems."

"What do you have in mind?"

"Well, all transporting of supplies and equipment for the naval fleet down there are contracted through the city. The city hands out contracts based on annual bids, but it's all a fucking joke, because Rossitello owns all the contractors who bid. So it don't matter, whoever the fuck gets the contracts."

"He controls the longshoremen, too, so how you figure to create union problems?"

Louie was in his element now. "The military don't allow no closed shop union, and even though it's rigged, one out of ten dockworkers are non-union. If Rossitello tries to force those guys to join the union, the Navy will cut him off and file suit. The port and the other big movers will be pissed off, because a lot of those guys go back and forth from job to job. Rossitello won't be able to get a job loading toilet paper on a fishing trawler."

"So you figure you can make it look like Rossitello forced the non-union workers to join up?"

Smiling now, Dragna said, "You just fucking watch."

Chapter 18

Lieutenant Dooley decided to do some investigating on his own and chase down a few leads that might be connected. Since his assistant was away at a law enforcement seminar, it was a good time for Dooley to do some freelancing, unencumbered.

He arrived at March Air Force Base, in Riverside, California, about midmorning. After showing his credentials, he was waved into the base, which was located on the edge of the desert. Early for his appointment with base personnel, Dooley took a self-guided tour of the facility. Although he had served in the Air Force, Dooley was never this close to the giant B-52 bombers he was watching while standing outside base operations.

"What do you think of March Air Force Base, Lieutenant Dooley?" an attractive WAF asked him when he went inside.

"Very impressive, Captain Wilson. It's been a while since I've been on an airbase, but I already feel at home."

"I've obtained the files on the airmen you requested, Lieutenant. I prepared a summary sheet which is the last page of each file. I'll let you have a little time to go over them. Then we can have lunch at the base cafeteria or the officer's mess, if you like. I recommend the officer's mess for quality, but the cafeteria for variety. Call me when you're finished."

Dooley spent two hours going through the files of Robert Tibbits, Andrew Crucianelli, and Arnold Redmond, after which he and Captain Wilson went to lunch. They elected to pick up a box lunch at the officer's mess and take advantage of the cool day in the park near the base chapel.

"I hope the reports provided the information you were looking for, Lieutenant."

"They did, thank you. Your summary was very helpful. As you pointed out, the fact that Tibbits, Crucianelli, and Redmond were each linked in some way to a black market operation during their time in Vietnam may be relevant."

"And if I may ask, what is your interest in these three?" Wilson asked.

"There's been a series of attacks on drug dealers in the LA area. The attackers rob the dealers, but throw the drugs away. It's kind of a vigilante type action, but of course, they do keep the money. At first the drug dealers were just getting rolled, but now they're showing up dead."

"And these three are involved?" Wilson asked.

"We believe so, but it's only two now, because Tibbits was murdered."

"Oh, my. That's too bad. I hope you find the guilty parties."

"We will, Captain. Having served in the Air Force, I personally feel bad about the path these three have taken. The other two may very well share the same fate as Mr. Tibbits."

"I hope not, Lieutenant. Is there anything else I can do to help?"

"I really appreciate the information you've provided. I'd like to give you one more name to check out. This man served in the Army, like Tibbits. How long would it take to get a report on him?"

"About ten days, same as before," Captain Wilson replied.

"That's fine. I'll write his name down for you. Call me when the report is ready...and regarding this one, I'd like to keep it under my hat, so please contact me directly when the information is ready."

80

"I will, and thanks for lunch, Lieutenant."

* * *

Cru, Red, and their captive had been staying out at the desert trailer for several weeks. Cru and Red took turns running into town for supplies and mail, or to attend to any other matters. Cru visited Christine every chance he got, but told her nothing about what had transpired.

Cru and Red weren't sure yet what they were going to do with their captive. His name was Juan Delacruz and he was originally from Guadalajara.

Cru was laughing. "How many niños did he say he had?"

"Seven little taco benders."

Juan told them he'd been recruited to work on the docks in San Diego. He typically loaded hundred pound sacks of flour in twelve-hour shifts.

"I bet that big beaner throws those sacks around like rag dolls," Cru said as he and Red went out to the shed to take Juan some food and get more information.

"Can you send my wife the money from my pocket after you kill me, por favor?" the man implored. "I rather die than live in this casa del chicken any longer."

"How come you kill people for assholes like Louie Dragna?" Cru demanded.

"I kill no one! The patrón who make me work no like me because I no kill. He send me to work on docks, to espia on Dragna. But Dragna catch me and tell me if I no kill you, he kill my wife and niños."

Cru and Red went outside the chicken coop and discussed it.

"That's the same thing Garcia told you, isn't it?" Cru asked.

Pablo Garcia was their contact in the Mexican mafia in LA. They met Pablo when they knocked over a drug dealer who had been abusing his wife. Pablo was with the dealer when Red and Cru robbed him, but convinced them he was a pawn and had no choice in working for the drug dealer.

He had since won Red and Cru's confidence and they exchanged information as needed.

Red nodded. "Yeah, it seems all these gangs prey on
the wetbacks that are just coming in. They blackmail them
into doing their dirty work. If they don't agree, the families get targeted." The two discussed it further and then
decided they'd take a chance.

"We're going to let you go, Delacruz. But if you rat
us out, or come back at us, we'll go after your niños ourselves." Cru threatened.

"No! I can't go back. You help me now," Delacruz said.

Baffled, Cru said, "We didn't kill you, and we're going
broke feeding your big Mexican ass. What the hell do you
want now?"

"They say they kill my familia if I not kill you. We
bring my wife and niños here...to safe place."

"Damn, we can't take care of your family, Juan!"
Red said.

"I take care of them. I work in farm field, in warehouse, anywhere. I can weld the metals, build the better
chicken coop than this basura...this garbage we stand in.
My wife, she cook, tend the chickens, wash the clothes...
anything you say," Juan told them, his eyes pleading hopefully.

"We'll think about it, Juan," Red said.

As they walked back to the trailer, Cru objected. "What
the fuck, Red? We're not running a daycare here. We got
enough problems without taking on all that shit."

"I know, but I was just remembering how we almost
left Hoa to the wolves. He tried to kill us, too, but look
how he had our backs after that."

"Well, we can't rescue everybody," Cru groused.

"Probably not," Red laughed, "but this one is
here now..."

* * *

"What the fuck is going on?" Angelo Rossitello demanded of the head of the San Diego longshoreman's union. A group of men identifying themselves as union reps had been systematically coercing the non-union workers into joining, sometimes by force.

The man cowered. "This ain't us, Mr. Rossitello. We don't know who's pulling this shit!"

"Bullshit! A bunch of union goons trying to shake down the hired help for a little extra dough. The Navy's threatening to cancel our contract, and now the goddamn feds are in on it."

"I called every steward in the union, Mr. Rossitello. I threatened them. Even put a bounty on whoever's pulling this shit."

"You trying to tell me that no one recognized any of these pukes?"

"No one! These fuckers must be some kind of agitators from back east." The union president sounded desperate.

Rossitello just glared at the man. Then it occurred to him: agitators all right, but maybe not from back east. Maybe somewhere much closer.

Chapter 19

"Any idea what this is about Sergeant Montrell?" his officer in charge asked.

"No, sir."

Doug Montrell had been summoned to base security at Wright-Patterson Air Force Base and was being accompanied to the meeting by his OIC.

"Guess we'll find out soon enough."

They pulled into the parking lot, went into the building, and were met by a uniformed major and a man in civilian clothing. They proceeded to a conference room with a telephone and speaker in the middle of the conference table.

"I'm Major Turner. This is Special Investigator Landrel. We're expecting a call from a Lieutenant Dooley of the Los Angeles County organized crime unit. He believes Sergeant Montrell may be able to provide information on some individuals possibly involved in malfeasance out there."

With everyone looking at him, Montrell said, "I'll do whatever I can, Major."

The phone rang a few minutes later and Major Turner picked it up. "Okay, Lieutenant, everyone is here. I'll put you on the squawk box." He flipped a switch, causing a short burst of static from the speaker.

"Good morning," Dooley said. "Sorry to have to bother you gentlemen, but this shouldn't take too long."

"No problem, Lieutenant, take as long as you need. Sergeant Montrell will answer any questions you have."

"Right, then, I'll get to it. Sergeant Montrell, during

your tour of duty in Vietnam, you bumped up against a black market drug smuggling operation, is that correct?"

"Yes, sir."

"Congratulations for your part in taking that operation down. I understand it was quite a hardship and that you have recovered from your wounds."

"Yes, sir, thank you."

"Sergeant Montrell, two of your associates during that time were Arnold Redmond and Andrew Crucianelli, is that correct?"

"Yes, sir."

"As far as you know, did either of them take part in smuggling weapons or drugs back to the United States, other than as ordered by Master Sergeant McKay, who as we know has been prosecuted for those activities?"

"No, sir. I witnessed no such activity."

"Did you ever hear of any such activity involving those two men?" Dooley probed.

"I did not, sir."

"Did you ever meet an Army sergeant by the name of Robert Tibbits?"

"No, sir."

"Before you were wounded, did Redmond or Crucianelli ever discuss their plans for the future with you?"

Montrell paused a moment. "I believe Andy wanted to become a tool and die maker back in Wisconsin. He was hoping to get an apprenticeship at a machine shop there."

"And Redmond?" Dooley asked.

"Arnold was hoping to get a degree in sociology under the GI Bill. He wanted to work in social services on the reservation where he was from, up in Minnesota."

"Did he ever talk about drug abuse on the reservation?"

"Arnold wasn't a big talker. But he did mention the poverty and the alcohol abuse he saw on the reservation. I know it bothered him a lot," Montrell answered.

"Sergeant Montrell, do you know where Crucianelli

and Redmond currently reside?" Dooley asked directly.

"No, sir, I do not."

The squawk box was silent for a short time. "Just a few more questions, gentlemen, and I won't take up any more of your time."

"Take whatever time you require, Lieutenant," Major Turner said.

"Sergeant Montrell, were you, Crucianelli, or Redmond ever solicited to become involved with the CIA or any other type of Special Operations details while you were in Vietnam?"

Montrell was surprised by the question. "Hell, no... Sir. As a matter of fact, it was CIA and Special Ops that tried to kill us. And they did succeed in killing several of our friends."

"I'm sorry for the loss of your friends, Sergeant Montrell. I think I've got all my questions answered for now. Thank you for assisting today, gentlemen."

"Call back if you require any further information," Major Turner reiterated.

"Thank you, I will."

* * *

The day after Juan Delacruz requested their help moving his endangered family from LA to Albuquerque, Redmond told Cru he thought they should do it.

"I don't know, Red. This guy could be setting us up," Crucianelli said.

"I don't think it's a setup. I'll take him to LA, and I'll play it safe. He still doesn't know where the fuck we are, and I won't tell him. He'll be blindfolded on the way there. Once we pick up his wife and kids, he won't try anything stupid."

Cru clenched his jaw and shook his head. He wasn't sold on the idea.

Red tried to assure him. "Look, I won't bring them here. I'll leave them in Placitas. They can set up shop and we can have Domingo keep an eye on them." Domingo was a neighbor in Placitas who did favors for Cru and Red on occasion. They found him to be competent and trustworthy.

Cru wasn't completely on board with the plan, but Redmond seemed determined to give it a try.

"That Mexican is pretty damn big. You're gonna have to keep a gun on him anytime he's not chained in the back of the van."

"Or a hose," Red interjected.

Cru laughed. "Okay, you crazy Injun. But if I don't get a call every night, I'll be looking for the circling buzzards."

When they got back to the chicken shack, they noticed Juan had somehow removed the handcuffs. Training his pistol on the large man, Red ordered him to sit down.

"They hurt Juan's hand," Juan said, pointing at the raw mark on his wrist.

"He bent these fuckers all out of shape!" Cru said, examining the damaged cuffs.

"Si...patrón." Juan sheepishly replied.

"Well listen up, Juan. We're gonna run you into LA. We'll bring you back to this area, but not to the trailer. You'll be shackled in the back of the van both ways. Your family will be in the back with you. No one learns the route either way. Once you're back, we'll be keeping an eye on you. If there are any problems, any at all," Red made a throat slitting gesture, "you're dead. Get it?"

"Si, gracias. Gracias, patrón. You not be sorry, I make no problemas. I help you any way you need, and my woman, too. Can we leave today?"

"We leave in two days," Red laughed.

* * *

"I can't thank you enough, Louie. How very thoughtful of you."

Mario Dragna's wife was going through the collection of rare porcelain that Louie surprised her with. The pottery, from the Ming Dynasty, was nothing short of spectacular.

Louie was in an effervescent mood. The plan to sabotage Rossitello's dock contracts had worked better than he dared to hope. After only one month, Rossitello's contracts had all but dried up. His other interests were suffering badly, starving for cash that was no longer pumped into them from the lucrative dock work. To compound Rossitello's problems, Dragna had allied himself with one of the San Diego Mexican gangs in a move to take over the dock working contracts. It would be years, if ever, before Rossitello recovered.

In addition to giving gifts to Mario's wife, Louie rewarded the associates who took care of the Rossitello business. He gave each of them a cash bonus and a top of the line Seiko watch.

Mario, however, still had concerns. "Congratulations, Louie, you've outdone yourself on this one. You've knocked Rossitello out and added another source of income to the business. I just hope you don't have a tiger by the tail."

Louie frowned. "Listen brother, you ain't gonna ruin this one for me. I didn't need your help taking care of it, and I don't need any of your snide remarks about it. If you have something to say, just say it or shut the fuck up."

"Okay, I'll say it, you hothead. Now you're in bed with the Mexicans. You think you can trust them? Killing each other is on their weekly check sheet. Some of them even have bounties on our heads: yours and mine!"

"I can handle the Mexicans."

"Really?" Mario challenged. "The gang you're in bed with is at war with the most powerful Mexican gang in LA. How do you think they'll react to this new partnership between two of their sworn enemies?"

Louie was taken aback. This surprised him in two ways. He was not aware of the feud between the LA gang and the gang he was collaborating with, and he didn't realize that his brother was so astute in his knowledge of their dealings. "How the hell would you know?"

Mario glared at Louie. "You think just because I spend my time on the commercial end of things, I don't know what's going on elsewhere? I make it my business to know all the details of every family enterprise. When we were just young punks, Pop told me I had to know where every penny went and every detail of every operation. He said, 'The day you stop doing that is the day you sign your own death warrant'."

Uncharacteristically, Louie was humbled and remained silent.

"Just watch those guys," Mario said quietly.

Chapter 20

"Well, you didn't expect him to talk, and he didn't. What's next, George?" Lieutenant Dooley and his supervisor were discussing Dooley's phone interview with Doug Montrell.

"I left the door open to call on him again. I'm going to keep after this Montrell. I think he knows more about his friends than he admits, but doesn't want to incriminate them."

"What makes you think he knows more?"

"Well, one of the items found in the apartment where Robert Tibbits lived was a small notepad containing letters and numbers. It was concealed in a corner of his clothes closet. The numbers turned out to be phone numbers, and we believe the corresponding letters are initials for the names associated with the numbers. Going over Crucianelli and Redmond's file, we learned of their close association with Montrell during their tour of duty in Vietnam. As you know, that prompted my interview with Montrell." Dooley explained.

"And you believe one of those numbers to be his?" Dooley's supervisor questioned.

"One of the numbers was adjacent to the letter M. The number was traced to a pay phone at a mall in Dayton, Ohio. Montrell is stationed at Wright-Patterson, just outside of Dayton."

"Good work, George. Keep me informed."

"Will do, sir."

* * *

After Red and Juan left for Los Angeles, Cru went back to Placitas to check for mail. A letter from Montrell asked him to call at a specified time and Cru placed the call from the mall payphone. Montrell told Cru about Lieutenant Dooley's questions.

"And he never mentioned Albuquerque or New Mexico?" Cru asked.

"No, he pumped me for your whereabouts a few times, but let it go when I gave him no real information," Montrell replied.

Cru was wracking his brain. "He must have spoken to a Tibbits family member. Damn, I wish I knew what they told him!"

"He said he might call me again at some point."

"You'll just have to keep stonewalling him, Monty. If he does call, let us know right away."

"Will do, will do." Montrell assured him. Shifting to a lighter topic, he asked "So what's with this fucking Mexican? You say he tried to kill you and now he's moving in with you? That hippie chick is making a pacifist out of your ass, Cru."

"Yeah, well Red feels sorry for him. Says he reminds him of Hoa."

"Well, I can see how, seeing as how Hoa wanted to kill us all at first, too. Just like this guy."

"And we wanted to kill him," Cru reminded Montrell.

The two made small talk for a while. Then Montrell asked, "You glad you got out, Cru?"

Cru thought about it. "I'm telling you, Monty, sometimes I wish I would have re-upped. That carefree life, three hots and a cot, and all that shit. But really, I like the freedom on the outside, and I like having a chunk of money in my pocket. But I sure miss you and Hoa and even that old buzzard Vodka Charlie."

They were both laughing now.

"I wonder how those two are doing," Montrell said.

"Well, you guys watch yourselves out there. Hope adopting this Mexican family doesn't bring you more grief."

"Thanks, Monty. Sorry you keep getting dragged into this shit."

"No sweat, I need a little excitement in my life. Pretty fucking boring around here most of the time." Just then, Montrell recalled another aspect of his conversation with Lieutenant Dooley. "Oh, hey! Speaking of Mexicans, you remember that big Mex from the First Cav that helped pull our sticks out of the fire in Nam?"

"Yeah, dude's name was Lopez. Funny you should bring him up. Red and I ran into him a while back in LA. What about him?"

"Right, Victor Lopez. Well, the last thing this lieutenant asked me was if I knew Lopez."

* * *

"What does this fucking gabacho want?" Rafael Tijenera asked.

As the head of Nuestra Propia, a powerful Los Angeles Mexican gang, Rafael controlled a large portion of the drug smuggling trade in Southern California.

"He says he knows who makes trouble for us in San Diego," a subordinate told him.

"Bring him in."

Alton Deem, looking haggard and scared to death, stepped into the fortified three-car garage where Rafael Tijenera conducted business.

"Why you bothering me?" Tijenera asked.

"Señor Tijenera, I lost my job because of what happened in San Diego with the dockworkers. But since I'm originally from Long Beach, I recognized some of the men who were making trouble there. I know who they work for."

"I know who you are, Deem, and I don't care about San Diego."

Deem took a heavy breath and continued. "The hombres taking over the San Diego shipping business have long arms. They are the compañeros of Louie Dragna."

Now Deem had Rafael Tijenera's attention. Stone-faced, he asked, "How do you know this?"

"Dragna and Rossitello have been fighting each other for years. I'm sure you know this. I was working for Angelo Rossitello when I lost my dockworker job. Before I lived in San Diego, though, I lived in LA and worked for Louie Dragna."

Chapter 21

As Lieutenant Dooley made his rounds, checking his contacts on the street, he bumped into an old adversary who was back in town. The man was coming out of a pawn shop that enjoyed a thriving business, thanks to petty thieves, burglars, and drug users. Dooley rousted the man and pushed him into the alley adjacent to the shop. A few vagrants scattered, although they did not have to worry, as Dooley was not interested in them.

"You got nothing on me, Dooley. Why you hassling me?"

"Alton Deem," Dooley noted. "You haven't been around for a while. Been sick?"

"Sick of your ass," Deem countered.

"I heard you moved to San Diego to get closer to all those Mexican whores you pay to screw. You miss us too much?"

"Miss you like a case of the clap, Dooley."

"I'm disappointed, Deem. After all the good times we've had together, you move twice and don't even send me a forwarding address. You want to go to the office or you going to give me some answers."

"To what questions? I don't know about any shit around here. I been working the docks down in San Diego."

"So I heard. Guess they had a few union problems down there, changing of the guard, so to speak?"

"I don't get involved in politics, Dooley. I do my job and collect my check. That's all."

"I understand you have some new friends around here as well. Really, Deem...Rafael Tijenera? Don't you know it's dangerous to play with snakes?"

"Better than rats." Deem shot back.

"Well, whatever you happen to be doing, I'm just glad you're back. I always like to keep close track of my good friends."

"Leave me alone. I can take care of myself."

Dooley left Deem with a warning. "Better take care of yourself better than your old friend Monk did. He ran into some very unpleasant people and it ended badly for him. Course I'm sure I don't have to tell you that."

* * *

Arnold Redmond and Juan Delacruz had stopped in Riverside so Red could have one of his contacts in LA do a little scouting before they drove in to collect Juan's family. He waited for the man's report before driving into Santa Ana to make the pickup. Delacruz had earned Red's trust and he rode in the front passenger seat, unshackled.

"I hungry," Juan said.

"Damn, feeding you is worse than that damn Cru. You guys should have an eating contest."

"Cru small, I win."

"Probably," Red laughed. "But we've had Mexican food till it's coming out of my ears. I'm ready for a steak and I know a good steakhouse out here, The Equestrian. We can have a beer and a steak, then camp out near the river. Tomorrow, if my buddy gives us the all clear, we'll get your family."

"I like steak," Juan said.

"I think you'd eat the north end of a south bound skunk, Juan."

"No, no, no. I no like skunk."

Red laughed again. "Okay, let's get that steak."

Red and Juan enjoyed their steak and a few beers, then parked their van near the river several miles from town. They laid their bedrolls under a partial moon and built a small fire.

"Reminds me of our campfires back home," Red commented.

"Si, me too."

"I got an old fishing rod in the back of the van and I bet there's some nice bullheads in this river."

Red got the rod ready, and Juan dug up some grubs for bait. They put the rod out and sat contentedly drinking their beer. Every now and then, they'd pull in a fat bullhead, which they put on a stringer and left in the water to stay fresh. They put the fire out and got in their bedrolls for the night.

After about thirty minutes Juan whispered, "Red?"

Red whispered back. "I hear 'em; let 'em get a little closer."

Red eased out of his bedroll and motioned Juan to do the same. Then they belly-crawled to the riverbank and waited. Red had his M-16 locked and loaded.

"Now!" someone yelled. Immediately a hail of gunfire erupted from a bush about thirty yards behind their bedrolls. The bedrolls took on life as they jumped around, riddled with bullets.

Red targeted the bushes where the muzzle flashes originated and opened fire.

Screams of pain erupted from the bushes. Red ejected an empty magazine and slammed in another. He carefully worked his way to the area, where he found an attacker who had taken several rounds through the chest and neck.

"One getting away!" Juan yelled, as he took off after a man who was running along the riverbank.

"Careful, Juan, he's still armed!"

But Juan had already caught up to the man, who was wounded and barely able to run. Juan overpowered him and beat him senseless.

Red caught up with them and said, "Don't kill the man, Juan. We need him to talk."

They dragged the limp body in front of their van and

turned the headlights on. In addition to receiving a beating from Juan, the man had taken a round through the calf of one leg.

Red walked up to the road and took a good look around for any other attackers. Just as he got to the shoulder of the road a vehicle sped away with its lights off. Red didn't risk taking a shot, but returned to the van.

"He okay," Juan said, as the man started coming around.

"Agua," The man moaned.

Seeing the man was Mexican, Red said, "You talk to him, Juan. Get what you can out of him." Juan started speaking to the man, who as yet was unable to reply.

"Agua," the man said again.

Red got a jug of water from the van and held it up. "Tell this prick he gets 'agua' when he tells us what we want."

Juan held up his hand. "I make him talk." He then spoke to the man in Spanish. After another minute of silence Juan put his big hand on the man's wounded calf and squeezed.

"Aiiiieeeeeeeee!" the man screamed.

"Digame!" Juan demanded.

"Por favor," the man groaned.

Juan squeezed harder. "Digame!"

Raising his hands in agony the man spoke in broken English, "I talk...I talk!"

* * *

Rafael Tijenera's subordinate, Chano, was tending bar in The Oak Room on a late night evening. Three of Louie Dragna's capos were having a party in the private room, celebrating their newly acquired management positions on the San Diego shipping docks. The men were drinking and shouting raucously, occupied with the activities of the five strippers who were dancing and entertaining them.

Chano quietly walked to the door, pulled the pins on two fragmentation grenades, rolled them along the floor into the party group, walked out the door, and closed it.

He drove a heavy bolt through a hasp, then sprinted out to a running auto, speeding away just as the grenades detonated.

Three of the eight people in the room died immediately. The other five lay screaming in pain from the metal fragments that pierced their entire bodies. Three of the wounded died before rescue squads arrived, and one more perished on the way to the hospital. The lone survivor of the ordeal, a stripper, remained hospitalized for months.

The turf war in Southern California was heating up.

PART THREE

"When we turn to one another for council,
we reduce the number of our enemies."

~ Khalil Gibran

Chapter 22

Dooley's supervisor called for a conference as soon as the report of the grenade attack on the Dragna party came in.

"Looks like the Crew struck back," Lieutenant Dooley's assistant announced.

Dooley's supervisor concurred. "I have to agree. This certainly seems like retaliation for those two Dragna killers that the Crew smoked out in Riverside."

"I'm not convinced this was the Crew, sir," Dooley objected. "From the information I have, these guys don't even have a presence in the area anymore. And as far as the Riverside killings, that appears to be an ambush gone bad."

Dooley's supervisor was getting impatient with the lack of progress regarding the turf war. "Then who do you believe is suspect?"

"Dragna sabotaged Angelo Rossitello's dock working contracts in San Diego. And now Rossitello has partnered up with the Mexican mafia here in LA. These guys all got a case of the ass for each other," Dooley said. "Even if the Crew were still around, they don't have the kind of muscle to pull off a stunt like that, nor have they been so inclined to do so."

"I think the effort to identify and flush out the Crew warrants more resources," Dooley's assistant, Sergeant Martin stated flatly.

Again, the supervisor agreed. "That's my opinion, too.

George, meet me in my office tomorrow morning at nine o clock."

"Fine," Dooley said, but his eyes were focused on his assistant who was walking out of the room right behind the supervisor.

* * *

Despite the attempted ambush in Riverside, Redmond and Juan managed to retrieve Juan's entire family and bring them back to Placitas, New Mexico, experiencing no further incidents during the trip.

"There's a passel of 'em, aren't there?" Cru noted as the Delacruz family settled into his and Red's bungalow. "Who the hell is the old lady?"

"She's the mother-in-law. Juan sprang her on me when we were loading up the van. I think we'll be staying out at the trailer a lot," Red conceded.

"So our boy in LA flipped on us, huh?" Cru noted, referring to their contact who had apparently informed someone of Red and Juan's presence.

Red frowned. "He sure as hell did. I thought for sure they were going to give it another try, especially when we picked up the family."

After the attempted ambush, Red and Juan drove to the far north end of Los Angeles and slowly made their way down side streets on their approach to the small house in the barrio where Juan's family resided. Once near Juan's home, they placed a call to Juan's cousin instructing him to have the family leave the house one by one and walk to the school where the children were enrolled. The ruse worked, and Red and Juan gathered each one up as they reached the bustling school yard. Juan's wife came last, with two small toddlers and the old lady.

Now back in Placitas, Red and Cru introduced Juan and his family to their neighbor Domingo. Domingo and his family agreed to help the Delacruz family get established, as Red and Cru prepared to head out to their trailer.

"Juan, change the head gasket on that van, and get it repainted like we talked about," Red said. "There are plenty of parts in the garage."

"Si, Señor Red. I weld stiffeners into frame, too. Van no wiggle after that. When you come back?"

"We'll let Domingo know when we're coming in. Make sure your wife and kids tell anyone who asks that you're just in from Mexico, comprende?"

"Si, they understand everything. They no talk about you or Señor Cru."

Before departing, Red and Cru left Juan and Domingo enough money for the Delacruz family to establish residency.

* * *

The attack on Louie's men in the bar had achieved several of Angelo's goals. The dock positions that became available were quickly snapped up by Rossitello's men under the guise of independent contractors. Shortly after the nightclub attack, two other Dragna capos abandoned their positions and went into hiding, allowing Rossitello operatives access to two more positions.

Louie was seething for revenge. Addressing his remaining capos and button men he growled, "This fucking bunch has got to be taken out! I don't care if it costs me a hundred large. You guys put a bounty on their heads and find them."

Only one man present had the stones to question him. "Are you sure it's the Crew, boss? I know our friends in the department are looking into that angle, but I'm thinking its Rossitello again."

Dragna was uncharacteristically patient. "The fragmentation grenades used to kill those poor bastards are the same type used all over Vietnam to whack officers and senior NCOs. This type of grenade ties it to those GI fucks that are making my life miserable." Dragna looked around a bit, then continued. "Besides, Rossitello has never directly operated in LA County."

The man was persistent. "But Mr. Dragna, so much weaponry has been coming back from the war these past couple of years, you could probably get a couple artillery pieces, a phantom jet, and maybe even an aircraft carrier if you tried hard enough."

Now Dragna looked directly at the young man, who dared to question his wisdom. "What's your name, son?"

"Bill, sir. Billy Falconnetti."

Chapter 23

Lieutenant Dooley reported to his supervisor's office as requested.

"George, you've been with us for several years, and up until now I've never had a reason to question your abilities or motives."

"And now?" Dooley asked.

"This business with the Crew has been going on too long. They've upset the whole applecart around here. We've got a full-scale Mafia war going on, and now the damn Mexicans are getting involved. When this Crew was knocking over drug dealers, everyone thought they were kind of cute. Sort of like a trained cartoon bear that beats up and robs the bad guys. But the bear has developed a taste for human flesh and is becoming very greedy. He needs euthanizing, George."

"Sir, I understand the frustration level here. And yes, my efforts haven't yielded the desired results. I'll pursue every avenue in flushing out the Crew, but I still believe the main perpetrators are the other parties you mentioned. In my opinion, they are the source of most of the violence we are seeing."

The supervisor took another tack. "That may very well be, but the ones that stirred all this shit up are the goddamn Crew, or whatever the hell they're called. Put the Crew out of commission and these other players will settle down and be content with the way things were before the Crew came onto the scene. Once the violence settles down, the public will settle down. When the public settles down, the mayor will settle down. And when the mayor settles down, then I will settle down. Understand, George?"

"I understand, sir. That may be the best outcome."

"You're damn right it is." The supervisor then took a conciliatory tone. "Listen, I understand your connection with these men, being from the military and all. I know you empathize with them, but we cannot allow our feelings to hinder what we have been entrusted to do."

"I'm sorry you feel I've let you down, sir. I will refocus my efforts."

"I'm going to make some changes in this investigation, and I hope they will be the solution to this problem. I'm going to ask you to dedicate yourself one hundred percent to identifying this Crew and once identified, to shutting them down." The supervisor then gave George a moment to consider it.

"What resources will I have, sir?"

"You will have unlimited funding, George. And the full cooperation of every department at our disposal. Do you accept these changes?"

George wanted more information on the resources he might have. "What about manpower?"

"You'll be on your own, unless you're in a situation that requires immediate backup, of course."

"Time frame?"

"Take as long as you need, but I prefer it be done quickly."

Dooley nodded. "I'll get it done, sir."

"Good to hear, George. I'm sure you won't disappoint me." The supervisor then looked intently at Lieutenant Dooley. "I'll also add that in my opinion, the best scenario regarding this...this Crew, would be termination."

"Termination, sir?"

Still looking at Dooley very intently, the supervisor replied, "Termination with extreme prejudice, Lieutenant."

* * *

Crucianelli and Redmond spent a week at their trailer in the hills near Albuquerque. They contacted Domingo every day, and he assured them that the Delacruz family was assimilating well. No problems of any kind had developed. The mother-in-law turned out to be an excellent weaver and began to share her skill with the other women in the neighborhood, bringing goodwill to the whole family.

Crucianelli made his regularly scheduled call to Montrell from the mall in downtown Albuquerque. After his discussion with Montrell, he headed straight back to the trailer to see Red, instead of visiting Christine.

"Monty says there's something going on. His buddy Vinnie Falconnetti isn't contacting him anymore or returning his calls," Cru told Red.

"Damn! He have any idea what's going on?"

"He thinks it's something to do with Falconnetti's cousin that works for the Dragnas. He hinted to Monty before that if something came up between his cousin and us, he might not protect us any longer."

"Fuck! If he gives us up, those pricks in LA could be drawing a bead on our asses real soon."

Cru paced back and forth, thinking. "We're going to have to move quickly. We should be okay here because the lease on this land and trailer is under Domingo's name. I think we'll have to close our bank accounts and empty the safe deposit boxes. Maybe open accounts in different banks with those ID's we finally bought."

"What about Placitas?" Red asked.

"Montrell's friend doesn't know where we are, to the best of our knowledge. He only knows our names. So we go back to Placitas and sell the house. We leave a forwarding address to bumfucked Egypt."

"Who do we sell the house to?" Red wanted to know.

"How about the current resident, Juan Delacruz?"

"And what happens when they trace us to our new residence in bumfucked Egypt, and we're not there? They'll

107

turn right around and come back here, try to flush us out," Red cautioned.

"Oh, we'll be there, all right. We'll be there," Cru informed him.

* * *

Louie Dragna invited Billy Falconnetti and his girlfriend to his desert retreat near Twentynine Palms, California, for a three-day weekend. Falconnetti and his girl were very much impressed by the Spartan beauty of the area, as well as the Olympic size swimming pool and the well-stocked bar and refrigerator. On the second day, Louie showed up with his mistress for cocktails and dinner. Louie cooked steaks on the grill, Sicilian style, for the evening meal.

"This is a beautiful place, Mr. Dragna. Thank you for inviting us here," Billy's girlfriend said.

"It is beautiful, isn't it?" Louie agreed. "I just wish I could spend more time out here."

The next morning Dragna's woman and Billy's girlfriend left for a shopping spree in Palm Springs, while Louie and Billy spent the morning trap shooting.

Billy admired Dragna's shotgun. "That's an amazing piece," Billy said.

"It's a Bennelli, from Italy. They just started making them a couple years ago. They used to only manufacture cheap motorcycles, but now they've managed to make a pretty damn good shotgun as well. I shoot every chance I get."

After a couple of rounds, Louie got to the business at hand. "So Billy, you don't think this bunch of fucks called the Crew is responsible for making my life miserable?"

"I do not, Mr. Dragna, I—"

"Lou," Dragna interrupted. "Call me Lou."

"Thank you, Lou. I believe the Rossitellos are creating a distraction so they can take over your holdings. A bad one, at that. There are twenty-seven incidents that can be credibly linked to the Crew. The money taken in those twenty-seven incidents amounts to less than four hundred thousand dollars. Chump change. Even if they sold the drugs they stole during those events—and everything indicates those drugs were mostly destroyed—that would only add another hundred grand or so to the kitty."

Dragna was impressed. It was obvious that Billy Falconnetti had done his homework. "Just petty thieves, huh?"

"Exactly my point, Lou. These are small time players. The fact that they haven't established any ties with the local Mexicans, the police, or even the fucking Boy Scouts, indicates they're just a small outfit, trying to make a score. I don't think they're in it for the long haul."

"So you don't think we should waste our time swatting these annoying pests?" Dragna asked.

"We absolutely have to focus on the real perpetrator of the recent misfortunes to your business, which I believe to be Angelo Rossitello along with his new allies," Billy Falconnetti replied. "However, this bunch, this Crew, needs to be taken out, and taken out quickly. You can't afford to have anyone damage your enterprise with impunity, Lou, especially a bunch of piss-ants like this."

Louie Dragna was fine with that.

Chapter 24

Lieutenant Dooley flew into Toledo, Ohio, several days after the meeting with his supervisor. He was now driving to Dayton, to meet with Doug Montrell in private.

Montrell recommended a nice steak house on the outskirts of town, and they met for a couple drinks at the bar during happy hour.

"I'm glad you decided to meet with me, Doug."

"Under the circumstances, I saw no other choice," Montrell replied.

"I was quite sure you were withholding information during our teleconference. I understand you want to protect your buddies. I was in the Air Force, too. Not in Vietnam, but I spent time in Turkey and a few of the other shitholes the Air Force always seems to find."

"They sure do find 'em," Montrell agreed.

Dooley got down to business. "Your buddies are in way over their heads, Doug."

Slowly nodding his head, Montrell agreed. "Yeah...I was hoping that after matching wits with the CIA, black market killers, and the fucking Vietcong, we'd come back home and take it easy. Looks like it's been anything but easy for some of my buddies. First they get spat on and get called all sorts of names, then they can't find work. No one wants to hire them, 'cause they think they're all druggies and killers. If they try to go to college the students avoid them and keep setting up protests. It's hard to study when all your 'friends' are burning the flag you served under. "

"I'm not going to ask you to incriminate your buddies, Doug, but you have to understand that there is no going back for them now. They've pissed off way too many people—powerful people on both sides of the ledger."

"I'm not sure exactly what you want from me, Lieutenant."

"Here's the deal," Dooley explained. "Your buddies unintentionally started, or I should say accelerated, a turf war between the two remaining Italian Mafia families in Southern California. As this turf war's been unfolding, a few snakes in the grass have been exposed. Some individuals who are paid to protect the interests of the citizenry have apparently been protecting some of these crime committing lice instead, all the while enriching themselves."

"What exactly can I do about this?" Montrell wanted to know.

"It's too late to keep your buddies from prosecution, but we might be able to keep them alive. That can only happen if you help and they cooperate." Noting Montrell's dour expression, Dooley continued. "We don't have many easy choices here, Doug. Are you interested in hearing my plan?"

* * *

Redmond and Crucianelli were sitting with their friend, and occasional business associate, Domingo. During their last call, Domingo had advised them to meet him at the Pueblo ruins near an ancient mesa. The three sat, sharing a few beers while enjoying the majestic scenery.

"Red brought the .22 because he thought he'd get a chance to pop a few bunnies out here. I'm getting tired of 'em, so it won't bother me if he doesn't hit any."

"I never miss, Cru. And you should be more grateful. Those rabbits make the best pasta sauce; your Aunt Tesla taught me that."

Cru had to agree. "That they do. So what's up, Domingo? How's the Delacruz bunch doing, are they repopulating again?"

"They're doing fine. Everyone gets along with them real well. That Juan can repair anything that's broke. And if he can't fix it, he's strong enough to cart it away on his back. He's the biggest damn Mexican I ever seen."

"Big as a horse, and eats like one, too." Cru agreed.

Red was laughing. "Cru's in danger of losing his title as the biggest hog in the west."

Domingo smiled and then got serious. "I brought you out here to warn you; you boys have a serious following in Albuquerque right now. Both times I went to your box at the post office some goons were hanging around giving me the fish eye. Then I went to the mall like you asked, to pick up Christine's car for Juan to repair. The same goons were hanging around the entrance of her store. I just skipped the pickup and left."

"Anyone follow you either time?" Red asked.

"The ones from the mall tried, but I ditched them at the interchange. I am very good at this. Before immigrating to the United States, I was an attorney in Mexico, practicing for the state and prosecuting drug dealers. When the drug dealers started threatening my family, I came here. But I know how to look over my shoulder."

"So that's how you learned how to come up with ID's and all that other shit," Cru commented.

"Without a license to practice in the United States, I had to find other ways to support my family. This is what I have learned to do."

"Glad you're on our side, Domingo." Red told him.

"Unfortunately, I have more bad news for you. After the incident at the post office and the mall, I did some investigating. In my field, I maintain many contacts who work on both sides of the legal system. I found two separate major threats facing you. One is coming from the Dragna crime family of Los Angeles. They've partnered with some Mexican gangs to hunt you down."

"Yeah, we kind of knew that and were hoping Dragna gets popped by one of the other bad guys. So who else is after us?" Cru wanted to know.

Domingo continued. "This one will be tougher to avoid, my friends: the Los Angeles County organized crime unit has also targeted you."

Red acknowledged that information. "Yeah, we heard they were investigating us from one of our friends that they interrogated."

"I have to advise you that the effort by this group has now changed from an investigation to one of termination," Domingo soberly told them.

* * *

Angelo Rossitello's consigliere had just dined at his favorite restaurant, Sottero's, in Riverside, California. He always said they made the best veal west of Chicago. The consigliere was in the company of two Rossitello button men and their mistresses. After dinner, they enjoyed drinks at the bar and then left to return to San Diego. In short order, they were pulled over by a California Highway Patrol car.

"What the fuck is this?" the consigliere asked. "We pay these assholes off, don't we?"

"They're on the payroll," one of the button men grunted.

The trooper approached and signaled for the consigliere to roll down his window. "License and registration, please."

"Officer, we represent Angelo Rossitello and we are here conducting business on his behalf. May I ask what the issue is here?"

"We just need to clear something up regarding the paperwork on this vehicle," the trooper told him, handing back the license and registration. "Follow me to the station please."

"What the fuck?" the consigliere said, but followed behind the trooper as ordered. Soon an unmarked unit pulled directly behind their car, hemming them in.

"Where the fuck they taking us, boss?"

"I don't know, but when Angelo hears about this shit, Barney Fife here is gonna get a real good ass-reaming."

After about fifteen minutes, the small convoy pulled into an old utility station off of the main road.

"This don't look like no kind of cop shop to me," the button man said. Two more vehicles pulled up on either side. The troopers in the cars ahead and behind left their vehicles.

Smelling a set-up, the consigliere flung his door open. "Fucking ambush!" he screamed, but before his door completely opened, several men with automatic weapons fired on the occupants in the trapped vehicle. Having little chance to react, and no chance to escape, the hapless members of the consigliere party screamed and thrashed about wildly as they were relentlessly riddled with gunfire. When the assault ceased, the vehicle was doused with gasoline and ignited.

Chapter 25

Lieutenant Dooley was still traveling when his supervisor met with Dooley's assistant to discuss the hit on the Rossitello party. The two occasionally got together in the supervisor's office and were meeting again in Dooley's absence.

"The Crew has been implicated," Sergeant Richard Martin reported. "The Rossitello party was killed with M-16's, all the brass was policed, and they torched the vehicle."

"Yes, Dooley's going to have a difficult time convincing anyone that these guys aren't responsible for all these killings we've had this past year. Once they're terminated, we can breathe easier."

Martin brought up a concern. "Do you think Dooley will terminate them, given the chance? I've staked my career on a successful outcome to all of this and we really need them out of the way."

"I think so. He understands the necessity of taking these vagabonds out. Once this is accomplished, changes will be made in the department. Your patience will pay off."

"I have to bring it up, sir. What if Dooley balks?"

Glaring sharply at Martin, the supervisor said, "Then we'll have to take matters into our own hands."

* * *

Red, Cru, and Christine were on their way to the trailer. Christine wept a bit as they left the metropolitan area and entered the stark landscape of mesa country.

"I'm sorry," she said. "I promised not to be a pain in

115

the ass and I'm already at it."

"You'll get used to it out here, and if things clear up soon, you'll be back in Albuquerque before you know it," Cru reassured her.

"I'm not crying because I'm unhappy, Cru. Remember, I grew up out here. I'm crying because I'm happy."

"The soul would have no rainbow, if the eye had no tears," Red noted, quoting a Native American proverb.

"That's a beautiful way of putting it. I've come to love you two more than anyone I have ever known. You've both shown me love, humor, strength, and kindness. So I don't want to become a burden to you. I'll carry my weight and leave if I become a nuisance."

"Now just wait a minute," Cru said. "I've looked at this damn Ojibwa every day for almost two years now, and believe me, looking at you in the morning will be much more pleasant than seeing his ugly mug."

"Me? Ugly?" Red couldn't let that go unchallenged. "Christine, I don't know how you can stand this fun-ny-looking dago. I've seen smaller beaks on old snapping turtles. And there are guys in prison with better disposi-tions. I think you only date him out of pity."

The mood lightened as the two bantered back and forth. Soon they reached the small back road leading to their trailer. The keen-eyed Redmond trotted in and checked things out, before they drove in and settled for the night.

* * *

Louie Dragna was on the balcony of his posh hotel room at Caesar's Palace, sipping an espresso. The Dragna family kept a room at Caesar's at all times, and Louie's mistress was inside taking a shower.

"There's that mean old bastard now, sitting there in his wife-beater tee, looking like fucking Caesar himself," the FBI agent commented. Local police had alerted the FBI that two men, believed to be Angelo Rossitello operatives, were in town, possibly stalking Louie Dragna. The police themselves heard it from casino management, who didn't wish to see one of their early patrons, not to mention best customers, come to harm.

"I don't get it. That asshole gets fucked by a hot babe and then has a nice breakfast, while we sit out here drinking cold coffee and eating gas station hot dogs," his partner groused. "Any sign of Rossitello's men?"

"No, and it's too damn bad," the other agent muttered, peering through binoculars. "They shoot that old bastard and maybe I could go home and see my kid's ball game for a change."

"What the hell, you want a life or something? Anyway, our relief should get here around noon. Where do these flatfoots get all these tips, anyway?"

The other agent scoffed. "These asshole mafiosos are like school kids. They snitch on each other all the time. They claim this code of honor bullshit, but violate it whenever it suits their own needs. Rossitello and Dragna are trying to get the cops...or us...to do their dirty work for them."

"Yeah, and from the scuttlebutt we've been hearing, the LA boys in blue are happy to oblige. I wonder what that's all about."

Chapter 26

Lieutenant Dooley returned from his cross country trip and was going over his report with his supervisor. Dooley thought they had always enjoyed an amicable relationship, but in the past few months things had changed. Today his boss seemed particularly formal and impatient.

"So as I understand it, none of your leads panned out, Lieutenant?"

"Not really, sir. I'm sorry to say both leads ran into a dead end."

"That's disappointing, George. Our department budget for out of state travel is precious, and it is very frustrating when no results are achieved from those expenditures."

"Sir, through the process of elimination, I will now be able to focus my investigation on the priority target which I originally identified as one of the Mexican gangs."

Dooley's supervisor was not in agreement with that plan. "I don't believe the Mexican gangs are responsible, George. They've become involved, but only out of necessity."

"Not gangs plural, sir. Gang, singular. I believe Nuestra Propia, the newest Mexican gang in the area, may have engineered this whole business, working alone."

The supervisor expressed skepticism. "I know these Mexican gangs are growing in size and scope, but I have yet to see a Mexican gang that has any kind of strategic vision beyond the next week. The type of planning and organized thought involved with the issue at hand reveals a detailed, highly disciplined, well executed process."

"They've learned, sir. They are shrewd and adaptive."

"George, the slash, smash, and grab tactics these guys employ are low maintenance and high yield. As much as I hate to admit it, it works. And they've done very well with it. Why would they move to a more complicated, high-risk venture?"

"Sir, those tactics are fine for thugs who are happy with garden-variety purse snatching, car theft, and drug sales, but if you're going to go for the gold, you need a strong organization and a good plan. And you need to minimize your competition. Typically, we'd expect Nuestra Propia to simply kill their competitors, but the local Mafia is, indeed, somewhat untouchable. For some reason they've been allowed to operate in Southern California for years, with impunity. Propia understands the local Mafia has special friends. So they work around it."

"What exactly are you implying, Lieutenant?"

"The Mob's been treated with kid gloves around here, sir. That special treatment has not gone unnoticed," Dooley told him.

The supervisor stood silent for a moment and then took a new direction. "George, I am going to make some changes to our organization. We need to refocus on what I believe to be the source of this problem, not what you or anyone else speculates. From now on Sergeant Martin will lead this task force. You will take direction from him, and you will turn over all investigative results to him. Is that understood?"

Dooley was not surprised. For weeks he'd had an uneasy feeling about the relationship between his assistant and his supervisor. He suspected his assistant of going behind his back, and now the supervisor was showing poor leadership in collaborating with him.

"Naturally, I disagree with this move, but I will comply with any order given," he told the supervisor formally.

"I understand your position, George. If at any point you feel too uncomfortable with this arrangement, it may be in your best interest to resign from the force."

"I understand, sir."

* * *

Cru was in Albuquerque, making his regularly scheduled call to Doug Montrell.

"I'm going to take some leave and come down there for a visit," Montrell informed his friend.

Cru was taken aback. "This isn't a very good time, Monty."

"Cru, we have to get together. I'm bringing someone you need to meet."

Cru wasn't too keen about that either. "Whoa, I don't know about that. Who is this person?"

"It's someone who has intimate knowledge of your activities...and your enemies. He's interested in helping you and Red extricate yourselves from the mess you're in. And he has the ability to actually do something about it."

Cru wasn't sold on the idea. "I'll have to discuss this with Red. We've been doing all right on our own."

"Really? Living with the Sword of Damocles hanging over your head, getting up every day wondering if this is the day you'll be killed? Scurrying around at night like a couple of scared rats? Is that how you want to exist?"

After a moment of silence, Cru conceded. "Look, I appreciate what you're trying to do. I'll talk to Red and call you back in two days. But I'll need some more information on this guy. Who exactly is he?"

Montrell told him straight out, "He's a cop."

* * *

Rafael Tijenera and two subordinates were meeting in their fortified garage headquarters. As the head of Nuestra Propia, Tijenera had been positioning Nuestra to replace the Dragna Mafia syndicate as the organization that had the connections in the police departments and court systems in the Los Angeles area. Some thought it a rather ambitious project when Rafael first made overtures to implement his plan. But Tijenera was not your average gang banger. He was a smart, forward thinking administrator who understood power and how to obtain it. He only lacked opportunity, but after implementing his plan that issue would be resolved.

"Our man in the department tells me there is a source of irritation in our plan regarding the Crew," Rafael told his subordinates.

Rafael had long since planned to kill the members of the Crew, but several attempts had been unsuccessful. Nuestra's tactic of carrying out robberies and hits, while implicating the Crew, had worked flawlessly. However, with the Crew still in operation, and even fighting back, things were becoming complicated.

"We were hoping the police department would have taken care of this problem by now. They accept our money, but do not complete their job," an associate complained.

"They do need to fulfill their part of the plan," Rafael agreed. "But we may have to lead this horse to water ourselves."

Chapter 27

Lieutenant Dooley requested a two-week leave of absence. Although his supervisor thought he'd requested the time to ponder his future, Dooley actually wanted to pursue his own investigation of the drug war. Working unfettered, without the prying eyes and interference of his assistant and supervisor, he might get to the bottom of things.

His first order of business was to meet with the two men he had discussed with Doug Montrell. He left word with Montrell that he was in Albuquerque and asked Montrell to have one of the two men call him at a pay phone near his motel at a specified time. He left the number and the time, and waited.

* * *

Although Montrell strongly urged Cru to meet with him, Cru was noncommittal. "I'll talk it over with Red. If both of us agree to it, we'll hook up with this guy."

Back at the trailer, Cru filled Red in on the discussion.

Red was understandably suspicious. "This fucking cop is in Albuquerque now?"

"He's at a Holiday Inn near downtown," Cru confirmed.

"Think it's a trap?"

"I really don't think so. Monty says the dude's all right. Says he's a straight shooter, ex-military and all that shit, figures he can help us."

"We've been shot at by plenty of military people who were supposed to help us," Red reminded him.

"Yeah, that's true enough. But we don't have too many

friends on our side of the ledger right now, Red. I'm think-ing maybe we should take a chance on this guy."

"Why don't we talk to him and then decide if we want to meet him," Red suggested.

Cru gave it some thought. "You know what we need here? We need a third party negotiator. We need a lawyer."

Red got the drift. "Domingo!"

"Yep. Let's go have a talk with our ex-lawyer Mexi-can friend."

* * *

One of Rafael Tijenera's lieutenants returned to LA after a trip to San Diego where he had gone in support of Rossitello regarding the shipping dock contracts down there. As Dragna's sworn enemy, Tijenera was backing Rossitello in the struggle for shipping dock contracts. The lieutenant, accompanied by several soldiers from one of his hit squads, stopped at a restaurant called Pablo's, then went to a nearby strip club which they often frequented. After the club closed, the men hung around in the park-ing lot, drinking beer and fooling around with the remain-ing strippers.

"You got any dope for us, baby?" one of the men asked.

"I might, if you ain't a narc. Are you?"

The men thought that was hilarious. "You ever see a bunch of Mexican narcs?" one of them asked.

"You can't be too careful these days, honey. I've seen them in all shapes, sizes, and colors."

A bit insulted, one of the men told her, "We are sol-diers of Nuestra Propia, and we kill narcs, like fleas on a dog."

"Nuestra Propia. Well okay, fella, come on over to my office," she teased.

The men followed her to an old semitrailer truck that was parked in a corner of the lot. She got a key out an un-locked the padlock on the back doors of the semi.

"You better have a bed in there, bitch. I always get

horny when I smoke," one of the men called out.

The eager men gathered behind her as she opened the doors wide. "Wait here," she said as she climbed up and walked to the darkened front end of the cavernous trailer.

A large spotlight turned on, illuminating the men standing behind the truck, then automatic weapons opened fire from the interior. Tijenera's men tried to run, but were cut down before they took more than one or two steps. After all of them were down, one of the attackers jumped down and shot each prone body in the head. The attackers then policed their spent shell casings and urinated on all the bodies before they climbed into the semi and drove away.

Chapter 28

Domingo contacted Lieutenant Dooley and met with him at a small bar on the outskirts of Albuquerque, where they now sat in a small corner booth.

"Cerveza, por favor," Domingo said to the bartender as he held up two fingers. He then addressed the man he came to see. "Lieutenant Dooley, my associates are busy in their import export business and requested that I meet with you during your visit. Please excuse their absence. As this letter indicates, they have empowered me to speak on their behalf."

"I understand, Señor...?"

"For our business, Domingo is all that will be necessary, Lieutenant."

"All right then, Domingo. Your associates' interactions with the drug dealing world of Southern California have had a major impact on the crime syndicates there. The activity of your associates, though insignificant in size and scope compared to the others involved, has created much turmoil among the competing large gangs in the area."

"What exactly have they been accused of, Lieutenant?"

Dooley humored him. "They've been accused of robbery, drug dealing, and murder."

"Isn't that what all the gangs in Southern California already practice, Lieutenant?"

"Yes, but they don't like competition, not from each other and especially not from a bunch of amateurs they believe to be working for one of the other gangs. This has set off all of them. Bodies are turning almost daily."

"Ah, drug dealers killing each other off. Isn't that what is called a win-win situation, Lieutenant?"

"In some societies, perhaps. But in our society in today's world, gun fights on the streets leaving bodies in their wake are not acceptable. I'll cut to the chase, Domingo. Strong evidence indicates that your two associates in the supposed import export business are the men known as the Crew. The Crew has been targeted for elimination by at least three powerful factions. I know they're in this area. And if I know it, I'm sure the others do as well. It's only a matter of time before they get flushed out by one of the bad guys."

Domingo considered the implication. "Lieutenant, if you are aware of this activity and know those who wish to bring harm to this Crew, why does law enforcement not put an end to it?"

Dooley looked away. "The reality is that at this time, there are elements in law enforcement—powerful elements—who for whatever reason also wish to see these men terminated."

"I see," Domingo replied soberly. "What do you suggest be done about this, Lieutenant Dooley?"

* * *

Later, Domingo met with Crucianelli and Redmond. Evening approached and the three men were out on the trailer porch.

Domingo started the conversation. "I believe this Dooley is a fair man. The news he brings is not good, but he has a plan to free you from the very real threat of death."

Cru and Red looked at each other.

"If he's a damn cop, why can't he just shut these guys down?" Cru asked.

Domingo pursed his lips. "Unfortunately, Señor Cru, the police are part of the problem."

Red didn't follow. "No comprendo," he said.

"Lieutenant Dooley believes that certain individuals—highly placed individuals—in the police department also wish to see you dead."

Red and Cru sat stiffly, not knowing what to think.

"I understand this is distressing for you, amigos. It is unpleasant to hear of such activity in a police department. This is why I left Mexico. The corruption and graft among the authorities there left no one certain of justice."

Red finally spoke. "You say this guy has a plan?"

"Yes, Señor Red, but it is not without risk."

* * *

"Fucking whore Dragna!"

Rafael Tijenera was enraged over the news that his best lieutenant and six of his soldiers were killed. "We strike back tomorrow," he ordered.

"Patrón, are you certain this was Dragna? We have many enemies who use many tricks," one of Tijenera's remaining lieutenants said.

"Who else? Who else would dare to do this to Nuestra Propia?"

Though reluctant to incur the wrath of Rafael Tijenera, the man pressed on. "Of course our desire would be to attack Dragna. That would seem only right. But we must remember who would benefit from such an attack. The murder of our compadres was perhaps meant to deceive us."

Staring attentively, Tijenera said, "Go on."

"The effort to make the attack appear to be by the Crew was very poor. I think whoever did this knew we would think Louie Dragna killed the men and tried to make it appear the work of the Crew."

The man got Tijenera's attention. "And who would benefit from an all-out war between us and Louie Dragna?" With a sharp look, he answered his own question. "Angelo Rossitello."

"Or perhaps certain members of the Los Angeles crime unit," the lieutenant suggested.

Narrowing his eyes, Tijenera nodded. "Perhaps," he said quietly.

Chapter 29

Andrew Crucianelli, Arnold Redmond, Lieutenant George Dooley, and Domingo met near Jemez Springs. The majesty of the Jemez Mountains impressed the small gathering.

"Beautiful country out here," Dooley commented.

"Perhaps not as grand as your Yosemite, but very magnificent, no?" Domingo replied.

"Yes it is. I don't get out to Yosemite as often as I'd like, sorry to say."

"That is a pity, Señor. Beauty purifies the mind, as they say."

"Yes it does, Domingo. Thank you for arranging this meeting with your compañeros." Addressing Crucianelli and Redmond, he continued, "Good to finally meet you men. I feel as if I already know you and sincerely hope we can resolve the problems you face."

"What exactly is your role here, Lieutenant?" Crucianelli wanted to know.

"I'm a member of the Los Angeles County organized crime unit, dealing specifically with drug cases involving organized crime. I am, or I should say I was, the officer in charge of the investigation involving the recent war among various factions of organized crime in the LA area. The suspected factions include the local Mafia, the San Diego Mafia, a San Diego Mexican gang, a local Mexican gang, some smaller Anglo gangs...and you."

"That's quite a laundry list you've got there, Lieutenant. We're pretty small potatoes compared to the rest of that bunch. So why are you focused on us?" Redmond asked.

"For several reasons. In every instance of murder in this ongoing war, the perpetrators of the murder have gone out of their way to make it appear as if you two committed the crime. A close examination of the evidence in those murders revealed slight variations which indicate that more than one of the factions is attempting to frame you. In other words, you two are the common denominator in all of this."

"You said 'several' reasons, Lieutenant," Crucianelli reminded him.

"You guys are on the hot seat," Dooley told him. "I know there have been several attempts on your life, and I strongly believe those attempts have been made by no fewer than three of the factions involved."

"That's two reasons," Crucianelli pointed out.

"I'll lay it all out for you," Dooley told them. "You two picked the wrong path to follow, but I think I understand some of the reasons you chose that path. And I think you can still get off that path and find a different one. In other words, I believe you're worth saving."

After Dooley finished talking, Redmond was curious. "You mentioned you used to be the officer in charge of the investigation, Lieutenant Dooley. If you are no longer on the case, why are you still involved?"

"I'm ex-military like you. And I'm tired of seeing our Nam vets insulted, belittled, and shuffled around, like some type of toxic trash that nobody wants to deal with; I don't want to see you two taken down."

* * *

The day after the meeting with Lieutenant Dooley, Cru and Red stayed in Placitas while Domingo went into Albuquerque to conduct some business on their behalf. He stopped for supplies at a supermarket, and proceeded to a liquor store. As he left the liquor store he was accosted by two men in the parking lot.

"I'll take that bag. You won't be needing it," one of the men told him.

After taking stock of the situation, Domingo said, "Go ahead. You must need it more than I do."

"We'll take the money bag, too," the second man chimed in.

"Si, Señores, take what you wish," Domingo said calmly.

After relieving Domingo of his liquor and money bag, the men ushered him into an alley behind the liquor store.

"You have all my possessions now Señores. Now please leave me in peace."

The first man then pulled out a large hunting knife. "We'll leave you in peace all right." He then plunged the knife five or six times into Domingo's torso. Domingo let out a short gasp, and slumped onto the pavement.

* * *

"Who the fuck are these idiots?" Louie Dragna wanted to know.

Dragna's capo held out his hands and shrugged. "They're a bunch of locals that call themselves The Minutemen. They were the only reliable people we could find out there. All the others we checked out were washed-up rodeo bums, drunk reservation Indians, or burned-out hippies."

Dragna viewed the man with narrowed eyes. "First, they kill some damn Mexican instead of the ones we're after, then they piss on him in a half-assed attempt to make it look like a Crew job. Whose fucking idea was that?"

"Someone thought it would be good to try to frame the Crew."

Dragna, a man with limited patience, was incredulous. "They were supposed to kill the Crew. How the fuck could the Crew piss on themselves if they had been killed? Don't you get it?"

"Hey, I don't blame you for being pissed, boss."

"Well, thank you. It's a real comfort to know that the morons I employ are sympathetic with me. No wonder Rossitello thinks he can roll over me."

"I'll go back there myself, boss. We'll get them," the capo said.

"That's a damn good idea. Make sure you get it right this time. Our organization and our very impatient friends in the department are counting on it."

Chapter 30

Dooley's supervisor and assistant were discussing the news from Albuquerque.

"Kind of strange," Sergeant Martin noted.

"Yeah. Our friends claim they weren't involved. I don't know if I believe them or not. Who the hell was this Domingo character anyway?"

"Apparently he acted as some type of counsel to the Crew. He was a prosecuting attorney in Mexico, but had to vamoose when one of the local drug kingpins put a price on his head."

"These Crew guys are harder to pin down than Jimmy Hoffa," the supervisor complained.

"If Hoffa had as many people after him as the Crew does, he'd have disappeared twenty years earlier. But anyway, why should we give a shit who kills them, so long as they're out of the picture?"

"Here's why. Our friends have a plan in place to consolidate the number of entertainment sector principals in the area. In order for this plan to unfold, they feel it is necessary for them to appear responsible for removing elements of lawlessness in that sector. These Johnny-come-latelys called the Crew have no allies around here. There is no one indebted to them for any reason. They hold no union contracts and have no friends downtown. They contribute nothing to the sector. They are expendable, but their disappearance must serve a purpose."

* * *

Red, Cru, and Juan were sitting in the back yard of the

Placitas bungalow, quietly drinking beer after they attended the memorial service for Domingo.

"I should have been with him," Juan said to no one in particular. Juan routinely accompanied Domingo, Cru, and Red on their inner-city business events. He had a shrewd eye, and because of his size and toughness, was a trusted, yet discreet bodyguard.

Shaking his head, Cru said, "Not your fault, Juan. Domingo should have waited for you. He knew better."

"Si, Señor Cru, but it does not make the pain go away."

"A good man once said 'It is not wise to listen to the cries of the dead'," Red commented.

Juan was grateful for the sentiment. "Thank you, Señor Red."

With his usual discretion, Cru broke the spell of the moment. "I keep saying Red's turning into a goddamn philosophizer in his old age."

All three men laughed a bit. Juan opened a bottle of mescal, tequila's tougher cousin, and proposed a toast. "To our friend, Domingo."

"To Domingo," they all said.

The three drank well into the night, finishing the mescal and the remaining beer.

* * *

Rafael Tijenera and Angelo Rossitello sat facing each other in a warehouse on a San Diego shipping dock. Although the two had formed a partnership to unseat their mutual enemy, Louie Dragna, the fact that they held no love for each other was obvious. Numerous men in the hierarchy of their respective organizations were also in attendance, eyeing each other uncomfortably.

"I'm impressed with your operation down here, Mr. Rossitello. I look forward to the day it passes to my hands."

"You are very confident, Rafael. Do you think you are capable of running such a sophisticated process? It's a bit more complex than stealing cars and beating up prostitutes," Rossitello jibed.

Smiling, Rafael said, "I think we will manage, Mr. Rossitello. But I think it necessary to eliminate our mutual enemy before we decide to face each other in the ring."

"Agreed," said Rossitello. "But back to the business at hand. Someone has been trying to kill these men known as the Crew. As we established in past conversations, these little amateurs have aided our mutual business ventures. Our friend Mr. Dragna, and his lackeys in the police department and courts of Los Angeles County, though inept, will eventually succeed. We must complete our endeavor before they manage to achieve their goal."

"Are you suggesting we intervene on behalf of the Crew, Mr. Rossitello?" Rafael probed.

"It may be necessary to provide them with a measure of protection until our plan is complete. Then, of course, we will deal with them accordingly. As I understand it, a group of local yahoos in Albuquerque, where this Crew now operates, has been engaged to remove them. One unsuccessful attempt has already been made."

Tijenera had the same information. "The group Dragna hired calls themselves The Minutemen. They are not much more than a drinking club with a few hunting rifles."

"That being the case, I am confident your organization can handle them." Rossitello remarked.

Rafael could give as well as take. "Certainly, Angelo. We will handle the tough jobs for you. This will allow you more time to drink anisette and eat the spaghetti which you are so obviously fond of."

While Rossitello bristled, the other Mexicans snickered. Rafael smiled at his own wit. "We must go now, Mr. Rossitello. I look forward to completing this phase of our business agreement." With that, he got up and walked out, all of his soldiers following behind.

Chapter 31

Lieutenant Dooley returned to LA, but didn't report to his office. Instead he called to arrange another leave of absence. Since his superior had let it be known that Dooley's presence was not required, or even particularly desired, Dooley encountered no problems extending his leave. When he heard that Dooley was back, a trusted friend in the department informed him of the latest developments in the case, including the murder of Domingo.

"That's a shame," Dooley said. "Domingo was a good man. Would have made a good prosecuting attorney somewhere, but was never given the chance." Since Domingo was the go-between for Dooley and the Crew, he would have to find another way to contact them. That problem was soon resolved, however, when he got a message to call an unknown number in Albuquerque at a specified time the following day.

Dooley placed the call from a pay phone the next day. Recognizing the voice on the other end of the line, he said, "Hey, Arnold, how are things going?"

"You tell me, Dooley. Shortly after we get together with you, our friend gets wasted."

"Red, I am deeply sorry about Domingo. I thought he was a class act and respected him for what he was, and for what he was trying to do on your behalf. But if you think I was responsible for his death in any way, you are deeply mistaken. I intend to continue to pursue the situation that has you and Andrew targeted for death, whether you believe me or not, and whether you work with me or not. But we have a better chance of resolving this issue if we work together."

"What do you propose now?" Red wanted to know.

"You guys stay in your safe retreat out by the mesa as much as you can. If your friend Juan can be depended upon, let him handle everything until this is resolved. I'll work through him if you vouch for him and arrange it. At some point for sure, we'll need to meet again. Whatever you do, stay away from the drug scene and for God's sake, don't try to avenge Domingo's death."

"Cru ain't gonna like that."

"Cru's a hothead, Arnold. You're going to have to be the cool one that prevails here. These guys are trying to flush you out. And they're getting close."

"I can try, but we'll need some assurance that there's a light at the end of the tunnel. Where is this going?"

"I'm putting together a coalition of support from law enforcement and civil authorities I trust. I have a pretty good idea who all the bad guys are now. We'll make our move when we think all the rats can be flushed out and caught."

Thinking ahead, Red asked, "What will happen to us?"

Dooley was brutally honest. "Worst case scenario, you'll be killed. Best case scenario is that with your complete cooperation, you serve a little time. If you get very lucky, you might get off with parole and time served."

"I'll talk to Cru," Redmond said.

"For both your sakes, I hope you convince him, Red."

* * *

After Red's discussion with Lieutenant Dooley, he and Cru went out to the trailer, along with Juan and Christine. Together, they made the decision to work with Lieutenant Dooley and arranged for him to visit. This time they'd bring Dooley out to the trailer. He could stay in an old popup tent trailer they had, as the existing trailer was already crowded. They told him to bring anything special he needed to eat or drink. Otherwise, he'd be subject to eating Red's rabbit concoctions.

Cru convinced Christine to permanently move in with them out in mesa country. She wasn't hard to persuade, as she enjoyed life out there much more than the life she led in the confines of her second floor apartment in Albuquerque. She donated all her furniture to a local commune and only insisted on bringing her dog and one cat.

Through Domingo, Red and Cru had already purchased the six acres of land the trailer sat on, putting it in Juan's name. Now they determined to build a ranch-style home on the land, as well as a large garage and a small barn. Juan and his family had originally lived in farm country in Mexico and were happy to move out to the country. Among his many talents, Juan was an excellent carpenter. A trusted friend delivered the building materials and Juan could be heard working on the new buildings from early morning to late evening.

"Are you going to loaf all day again?" Red asked Cru.

Cru had been standing around, watching the industrious Juan laying out the building site. Red was assisting him.

"Hey, I'm the jefe of this outfit. Someone has to make sure you guys don't mess up too much. I also have to make sure the beer is cold."

"Jefe, my ass," Red said. "Juan's wife works harder than you do, and she's pregnant."

"Again? I don't see how Juan finds the time, with all the shit you make him do. Maybe we're going to see a little papoose come out of there, instead of another little chico," Cru baited.

Red wouldn't let that ride. "Well, if we need another Italian around here Christine will probably have to send for one of the Dragnas, as lazy as your ass is."

"The Dragnas are old, Red. Christine likes young men," Cru retorted.

"Does she like lazy men, too?"

* * *

Mario and Louie Dragna were sitting on Mario's patio sipping grappa after Mario had invited Louie and his mistress for dinner. Mario's wife didn't approve of the Italian male's habit of keeping two women, but she actually liked Louie's girlfriend better than his wife, so she hadn't objected to the invitation her husband extended.

"You know that Fat Angelo has teamed up with the Mexicans," Mario said flatly.

Louie snickered. "They call themselves noostra something or other. Bunch of fucking car thieves and pimps. They work out of a taco wagon in Alhambra. Rossitello must need a few decent leg breakers. His are all old and fat like him."

Mario was shaking his head. "Nuestra Propia has a fortified three-car, two-story garage in Anaheim for headquarters. A significant source of their income is from drugs, but they're also involved in horse wagering, trotters mostly. They own seventeen massage parlors in Los Angeles County and twenty-five auto repair shops."

With a look of surprise on his face, Louie stared at Mario. It seemed he had underestimated his brother again.

"Know thine enemy, Louie," Mario reminded him.

"Okay, what do you suggest we do about it?"

Mario had an idea regarding that also. "I'm sure if our friends downtown were aware of this new partnership, they would make life very difficult for these criminal collaborators."

"Maybe they already know."

"Perhaps, but it is possible they don't realize the negative impact this union of snakes will exert on our business interests. We pay a king's ransom for protection from this type of activity. We must let them know we expect their involvement when it is needed."

It was Louie's turn to smile. "Big brother, you surprise

me. You always preach about never letting an opportunity slip between your fingers."

"What are you getting at?" Mario wanted to know.

"Did you ever hear of Joe Masseria?" Louie asked.

"No, who the hell is he?" Mario wasn't accustomed to being outsmarted by his brother.

"Joe Masseria and Salvatore Maranzano were bosses way back in the thirties. Masseria was a wise guy from the States, while Maranzano represented Sicily. They originally had a partnership, but it was doomed to fail from day one, and they were soon killing each other off. Maranzano appeared to have beaten Masseria's clan, but some upstarts jumped in and kept the war going. Took the starch out of both of them. The upstart who kicked the most ass took over the whole enchilada, so to speak. His name was Lucky Luciano. I'm sure you've heard of him."

"I'm impressed, little brother. I gather you're suggesting we hold off and let the natural evolution of things take place?"

Louie nodded. "Yep, this love affair won't last long, I assure you. They'll wear down and start squabbling. And the cops will be running them ragged the whole time. When one party is knocked out, and one weakened party is left, we move in and clean up."

"Well, I have to agree with that thinking," Mario told him.

Louie nodded. "An old paisano once said, 'Never interrupt an enemy when he is making a mistake'."

"Damn good advice, Louie. Who said that?"

"A Corsican whose family was originally from Tuscany: Napoleon Bonaparte."

Mario sat quietly, shaking his head and smiling. He certainly had underestimated his little brother.

Chapter 32

Lieutenant Dooley arrived in Albuquerque three days after he spoke with Crucianelli. He flew in late in the evening, picked up his luggage, and met Juan at the passenger pickup area.

"Thanks for picking me up, Juan. Even though we haven't met, I feel as if I know you from my discussions with Red, Cru, and Domingo."

"Si, Señor Lieutenant, I have heard much about you, also. I am glad you are helping us with our problem. Red and Cru are good men. They were breaking the law by robbing drug dealers, but also help people with the money... and with their hearts, also."

Dooley's trained eye picked up a vehicle that had followed them onto the freeway. He watched their movement in the rearview mirror for a few moments. "Stay in the right lane and get off at the next exit, Juan. Don't use your turn signal and wait until the last second to exit."

Alarmed, Juan looked at the rearview mirror. "What do you see, Lieutenant?"

"A delivery van that was parked behind you at the airport is following a couple hundred feet back in the middle lane."

After several minutes, the next exit appeared. Juan waited until the last possible moment and pulled off the freeway. The delivery van attempted to follow, but was hemmed in by another vehicle in the right lane and missed the exit.

Dooley watched over his shoulder. "They didn't make

the exit. Good work, Juan. Can you take a different route to the trailer?"

"Si, Lieutenant, I know many ways. They will not find us again. Soon we get to our trailer and have a nice Cerveza."

"I believe I'll have more than one of those, Juan. And just call me George."

* * *

Juan and Lieutenant Dooley got in very late and informed the others about the incident with the delivery van. Then they had a quick beer and went to bed. Juan was up early, working on the new ranch house, so Crucianelli and Redmond drove into town for supplies.

"Kind of lost without Juan," Cru commented.

"Yeah, he has been on every road trip lately. Guess we'll have to do our own singing, and you'll have to double up for him at the all-you-can-eat buffet. Something you're good at."

"Nah. I hate to admit it, but that man can put me to shame. The other night he ate seven tacos."

"You must have had a stomachache. You normally eat about ten. But at least I don't have to listen to you sing."

"I can sing," Cru protested. "I just don't know any damn Injun music, even though I could beat on a drum for three hours straight if I wanted to."

"Why don't you sing me some opera?" Red asked.

"If you remember, old Vodka Charlie asked me the same damn thing when we were in Nam, and I'll remind you what I told him then. Good singing would be wasted on you guys. Some out-of-tune hillbilly music would be more to your liking."

"Well, not me," Red laughed. He looked at the list of items Juan had asked for. "Damn, Juan's got everything on here but a mariachi band. Good thing we got the van."

"That ranch house is going to look like the fucking Taj Mahal when he gets done with it. We're going broke feeding that damn Mexican and his forty kids, and now he's gonna break the bank building a hacienda for them all."

"Well, with the way you and Christine go at it, he's probably figuring there'll be a bunch of short bow-legged runts crawling around wearing hippie beads real soon."

"My kids ain't gonna be no damn hippies," Cru protested.

"I notice you don't deny they'll be runts, though. You know, Cru, I've seen squaws taller than you," Red taunted.

"And I've seen squaws skinnier than you, just can't remember when."

The two bantered back and forth for most of the morning as they went about their business. They kept an eye out for suspicious activity, but were not harassed or molested during their trip. They picked up everything on Juan's list, restocked their ammunition at a sporting goods store, and then picked up more beer at the liquor store.

"That damn Dooley drank a twelve-pack the last time we got together. We better keep him supplied or he'll turn us over to the Feds," Cru advised.

"Well, if he doesn't sing when he's drunk, that'll be an improvement," Red commented.

"I thought you liked my singing?"

"It's like a bad commercial. It sticks in your head and you can't get it out."

* * *

"We have confirmed that the two men we are looking for are in Albuquerque," Rafael Tijenera said into the phone.

"If you know that, why didn't you take care of the problem?" Angelo Rossitello wanted to know.

Tijenera braced himself. "The vehicle they were in managed to evade our men. They got a good description and plate number, though."

"That's worth two dead flies, Tijenera. These guys probably change their plates more often than you change

143

your underwear. Do I have to send my guys out there?"

"Only if the Crew are in need of someone to deliver a pizza," Tijenera fired back.

"A fucking pizza driver wouldn't have lost those bums," Rossitello said.

"If you wish to take over the task of handling this problem, Angelo, we will be glad to let you do that. Give me the names of your contacts inside the department, so we can assume that responsibility."

Rossitello was now enjoying himself. "You guys would probably fuck up the information and call the fucking DA by accident."

"If you can dial a phone with your fat fingers, I'm sure we could manage somehow."

"It won't happen, Rafael. Our contacts in the department are not going to deal with any tomato pickers. They have all the produce they need, and if they have to use a translator, they'd just as soon speak to an Oriental, or someone who can offer something of value."

Tijenera was now seething. "When this is over, you and I will settle up personally, Angelo."

Chapter 33

Red, Cru, Juan, and Lieutenant Dooley sat at a large folding table in the newly constructed barn. The interior was unfinished, but the shelter afforded them a measure of privacy, as well as relief from the unrelenting sun.

Dooley, who had some organizational charts made up, began the conversation. "There are two main coalitions we have to deal with. San Diego Mafia Don Angelo Rossitello has allied himself with Rafael Tijenera, the head of Nuestra Propia in Los Angeles. Their goal is to replace the Dragna Mafia family as the top organized crime family in LA. In order to do that, they need to displace the Dragnas as the ones who have the powerful connections in the LA police and judicial system. Meanwhile, the Dragnas have allied themselves with some up and coming Mexican gangs in San Diego."

"Why are they so interested in us?" Red wanted to know.

"Because each one of them believes you are allied with their opponent. Ironically, evidence of the killings in which you were implicated shows that half of the killings appear to have been carried out by one of the coalitions, and the other half by the opposing coalition."

"So we're the big, bad bogeymen," Cru said. "Too bad the police won't just go in and bust them all up."

Though somewhat uncomfortable now, Dooley continued. "The fact is, there seems to be a high level of police complicity with each of the two coalitions. Both of them have highly placed individuals on the force. I suspected collusion from certain individuals in my own department. I approached other trusted individuals with my suspicions, and an investigation began. Because of the high rank of some of the suspected individuals, we have had to be very thorough, very sure of our findings."

"How many from the police force are involved?" Red wanted to know.

"It appears to be at least a half dozen. We brought the FBI in right away. They took one of the individuals into custody and he agreed to work as an informant for a reduced charge. The FBI is hoping to keep the case an active investigation until they're absolutely certain all the rogue police are identified."

"What do they know about us, and what is their intention?" Cru wanted to know.

"The FBI tends to deal in absolutes. You're either a good guy or a bad guy."

"No sensitivity, huh?" Cru noted.

"They're not exactly the touchy, feely types," Dooley acknowledged.

"And the cops are," Cru remarked.

Dooley overlooked Cru's sarcasm. "I believe the team we have in place is capable of resolving the serious issues we are all facing, in the most suitable fashion possible."

"Are they aware that you are in contact with us?" Red asked.

"No," Dooley said. "Again, because of their size and scope, the FBI doesn't deal with the human aspect of things very often. They crunch numbers, identify targets, and take them down. When the time is right, they'll be informed of our relationship. Hopefully, by then your lives will no longer be at risk."

* * *

Christine had errands in the city and was accompanied by Juan while she tied up some loose ends. She picked up her mail and set her new forwarding address as a post office box Cru had provided. Then she went to the boutique at the mall and informed her manager that she was quitting her job. Juan sat out in the middle of the mall munching caramel corn while he waited.

As Christine emerged from the boutique, two men grabbed her by each arm and forced her to go with them. No wilting wallflower, Christine kicked and screamed while the two men tried to hurry her to a nearby escalator. Passersby stopped and watched, astonished as the scene unfolded.

Just as the struggling trio got onto the escalator leading to the lower level, Juan caught up with them. He grabbed one of the men from behind, locking his huge left arm around the man's throat. As the other man released Christine in order to fight off Juan, Juan's right fist crashed down on the top of his head, knocking him senseless. The momentum of the blow sent the man over the escalator rail, and he plummeted to the first floor, landing like a sack of potatoes.

Still holding the first man, who was now turning blue and choking, Juan delivered his right fist to the man's head. The man's eyes rolled up and he slid down the escalator stairs, crumpling into a heap at the bottom. Juan and Christine followed him down, stepped over him, and quickly exited the building. After they left the parking lot and moved out of the vicinity of the mall, Juan turned to Christine.

"Are you all right? Did they hurt you?"

"I'm okay. A little shook up, maybe. I'll probably have to stop and pee somewhere."

"I think those men are lucky I saved them from you," Juan teased. "You were giving them a good beating."

Christine could now laugh as well. "Well, those bastards thought I was an easy mark, but my father didn't raise any sissies. I figured whatever they were gonna do, I'd make them pay for it. Thank God you were there, Juan. Thank you for saving me."

"I think we both give them a good lesson, Señorita Christine."

* * *

Louie and Mario Dragna were having a bit of fun at Angelo Rossitello's expense.

"Fat Angelo and his new beaner buddy are a fucking riot. They tell me there are millions of brilliant people in the world, but I guess none of them work for those two dumb bastards," Louie said.

"Well you sure called that one," Mario told him. "Those two couldn't catch the clap in a Tijuana whore house."

"It won't be long before they're killing each other, I promise you that."

"Who's this new whiz kid you've been talking about anyway?" Mario asked.

"His name is Billy. Billy Falconnetti."

"Falconnetti?" Mario said. "Any relation to Vinnie?"

"He's Vinnie's cousin. Came out here last year. Damn smart kid. I'm thinking that once we decapitate Fat Angelo, this kid could become our guy in San Diego."

"I'm sure Angelo's going down, but it may be at the hands of his current partner. We're going to have to figure out how to deal with Tijenera, regardless of who takes Rossitello down. He's the smarter of the two, and his power grows every day."

"What have you got in mind?" Louie asked.

"What Tijenera wants more than anything else is our connections in law enforcement and the judicial system. We have to acknowledge that due to the rapidly changing demographics in Southern California, the 'entertainment' segment of our business will eventually pass into his hands."

"Are you suggesting we give in to this motherless fuck?" Louie demanded.

"We have to face reality, Louie. Every time a Mexican woman in Southern California has a baby, Tijenera's power increases and ours decreases. And every time a Mexican hops over the border, the same results occur." Mario then leaned in close. "To ignore this is to ignore that the earth is round. We can fight it and go down, or we can try to find a way to deal with it. It's in our best interest to learn how to deal with it."

Chapter 34

Dooley, Crucianelli, and Red sat at the folding table in the new barn. The framing of the ranch house was almost complete.

"Damn good thing Juan was with Christine," Dooley remarked. "Very glad she didn't get hurt."

Cru agreed. "Juan is worth his weight in gold."

"Well, maybe half his weight," Red noted.

Cru laughed. "Yeah, maybe half, Red. This was more of those Minutemen, I take it?"

Dooley nodded. "Yes. I believe Rossitello hired these guys. Or his partner Tijenera."

"You can link them, Lieutenant?" Red asked.

"The one who was killed when he fell off the escalator had a notepad in his pocket. The writing on one page included a monetary figure and a set of initials. The initials were A.D."

"That means something to you?" Cru asked.

Dooley nodded. "A long-time LA drug dealer and garden variety scumbag known as Alton Deem was known to have ties to organized crime, specifically the Dragnas. Apparently Deem and the Dragnas had a falling out as a result of the recent goings-on, and Deem defected to the Rossitello camp. Rossitello and his associate Rafael Tijenera have given him shit job after shit job. And this smells like his work."

Dooley noticed Crucianelli and Redmond now looking at each other. "You two know this guy?"

Cru nodded. "Deem is the lowlife that had Bob Tibbits killed."

"How do you know this?" Dooley asked.

Although Cru was aware of the relationship between Dooley and Montrell, he would not drag Monty into it any more than he already had. "One of our contacts in LA fingered him," Cru said.

"Really?" Dooley said, with a hint of doubt in his voice. "May I interview this person?"

Crucianelli was coy. "He's not an easy guy to get hold of. Pretty skittish. Not sure he'd talk to a cop. If I put you on him, it would probably fuck our situation pretty good."

"And how's your situation now, Andy?" Dooley asked.

* * *

Louie Dragna and his consigliere were in San Diego, meeting with the head of the Mexican gang that was taking over Rossitello's territory, little by little.

"Do you think you can find these two assholes in Albuquerque that our enemies wish to kill?" Dragna wanted to know.

"Si, I can most certainly do that. But why not just let our enemies kill them? When they finally manage to complete their job, our only job is then to kill Señor Rossitello and his little toad Rafael, no?"

"There is a complication now. A police lieutenant has allied himself with these two piss-ants in Albuquerque. Any attack on them is likely to involve him. Harming a policeman is a messy business."

"Señor Dragna, you are a modest man. Your connections with the police force are many, and powerful. Surely they can pull the leash of this stray dog and bring him back to his kennel."

Dragna explained his reasoning. "This overzealous lieutenant may have put himself in danger, while at the same time performing a service for us. It is my belief that our incompetent friends will soon succeed in their attempt to take out the Crew. This unfortunate police officer may also be killed in this tragic event. Evidence of the many past attempts on the lives of the Crew by Rossitello and Tijenera will certainly come into police possession during the course of their investigation. And we will be rid of them all."

Louie's associate smiled. "I understand, Señor Dragna."

Louie was now smiling also. "Let's make it happen, compadre."

* * *

It was the third Tuesday of the month, the day Dragna normally conducted meetings with several key associates. The meeting was in full progress and the security man was idly standing by his station inside, smoking a cigarette and paging through a girly magazine. Alton Deem, wearing his old security uniform, stood outside Dragna's warehouse. After looking around, he walked through the door.

"Hey," The security guard said. "What's up?"

"We've got a new locker for this building. Can you give me a hand carrying it in?" Deem asked.

"Sure, I guess. What's wrong with the old locker? Seemed okay to me."

Deem held out his hands. "The super says everyone keeps breaking into them and pilfering, so all of them are getting replaced."

The security guard followed Deem to the back of the van. Deem opened both rear doors and while the guard was looking the other way, removed a slapjack from his pocket and whacked the man over the head. After the man fell to the pavement, Deem pulled out a .38 Smith and Wesson with a suppressor on it, shot the man in the head, and pushed him under the van. He then went back into the building and sat in the security guard's chair.

After forty-five minutes the men started ambling out of the meeting room. No one took notice of Deem as he sat, seemingly buried in his magazine. Always the last one to leave, Louie walked out about ten minutes after the last man had left. He took one look at Deem at the security desk and stopped abruptly.

"What the fuck?" Dragna yelled.

Deem dropped the magazine, raised his .38, and shot Dragna in the head. As Louie slumped to the floor, blood gurgling from the exit wound, Deem shot him two more times in the chest, urinated on his body, and left the building.

Chapter 35

"We need to come up with a plan," Dooley's supervisor told Sergeant Martin. They were now dealing with the reality that their benefactor and associate, Louie Dragna, was dead.

"We better come up with something pretty damn quick. Rossitello and Tijenera may have other shit already in the works," the assistant advised.

"This isn't the only problem we have. Dooley rounded up some kind of half-assed posse, and people have started asking a lot of questions. That sonofabitch has got everyone but the Boy Scouts sniffing around here. Our buddy in the DA's office won't hang on long if there are federal subpoenas involved. He'll throw us to the wolves."

The aide was understandably worried. "This thing hasn't exactly turned out the way we expected. Maybe we should talk to the DA ourselves, before the whole damn thing blows up."

"Let's try to think this through logically," the supervisor cautioned. "If something does happen, they'll throw the book at me. I'll lose everything I've ever worked for: my family, my status in the community, and my pension."

The assistant didn't like where this was going. "What are you suggesting?"

The supervisor took a breath. "You're a young guy, without much experience...or much to lose. If you claim the Dragnas coerced you into all of this, you'll probably get off with a very light sentence, maybe even probation." He was trying to sound hopeful.

"You're asking me to take the rap?"

The supervisor struck a conciliatory tone. "I'll do everything I can for you. I'll pull as much weight as possible to lessen the sentence. And when you get out, your share will be waiting for you. You'll be able to start a new life doing anything you want."

Looking at his supervisor with narrowed eyes, the man asked, "Exactly how much would that share be?"

* * *

Although he was dead, the mission Louie had authorized to take out the Crew and the police lieutenant allied with them was still in progress.

On an early crisp morning, Andrew Crucianelli and Juan's oldest son Abel were heading to the barn to check on a mare that was overdue to foal. Redmond thought he'd check on the mare as well, and left the ranch house a minute after Cru and Abel. The keen-eyed Ojibwa immediately caught the reflection of sunlight from two shiny objects in the foothills directly overlooking their ranch. Looking back toward Cru and Abel, Red yelled, "Take cover! Take cover!"

Startled, Cru started to turn around, just as two heavy-caliber weapons opened fire. As he turned, one round passed directly through the leather oat bag he was carrying, spinning him around like a top. Abel, now looking up, took a round through his shoulder that sent him flying like a rag doll.

Crouching and running toward the stricken men, Red grabbed the oat bag handle and dragged Cru into the barn. The momentum from the shot that Abel had taken carried him behind some heavy equipment, leaving the shooters with no good targets.

Hearing the shooting, Juan stepped out of the ranch house back door with an M-16. He took a good look around before running to his son, who was now lying prone behind the equipment. Shots again rang out as the attackers attempted to hit Juan. Red made sure that Cru was all right and arrived to help Abel at the same time Juan arrived.

"Where are you hit?" Red asked.

"Just inside my shoulder," Abel grunted.

"Keep us covered, Juan." Red opened Abel's shirt and checked the wound. "Not bleeding too bad. Looks to have passed clean through between the shoulder and the rib. Damn large caliber weapon, though. Gonna need a lot of stitching up, inside and out. Can you move?"

Abel nodded.

"We'll get around the other side. You lay out some cover fire, and I'll take him," Red instructed Juan.

At Red's signal, Juan started spitting M-16 fire at the two positions Red showed him. Abel got to his feet, leaning heavily on Red, who directed him between the equipment and the shed, and took him around back into the ranch house.

Juan's mother and Christine took Abel and got him into the safe room Juan had incorporated into the floor plan per Cru's instructions. It was a large stand alone room in the middle of the house. The walls, which had separate concrete footings, were made of six-inch reinforced concrete with quarter-inch boilerplate steel encasing them. A pump brought air in from a hidden duct that ran several hundred feet behind the building. The room included a ventilated porta-potty and enough food and water to last a dozen people for ten days.

After making sure everyone in the house was in the safe room, Red grabbed another M-16, some additional magazines, and ran back to Juan's position behind the equipment.

"Thought I told you to stay put."

"You always try to leave me out," Cru complained.

"If I needed a bad shot, I would have sent for Sergeant Prentice."

Looking toward the now quiet hill, Red said, "We're

going to have to get above them."

"What the fuck are they shooting, buffalo guns?" Cru asked.

"Judging by the sound of them and Abel's wound, I'd say a .338 Win-Mag," Red told him. "They've got scopes, so we don't want to give them any kind of target for very long."

"Which one you want me to take?" Cru asked.

"Neither. That arm of yours is injured. You'd shoot even worse than you normally do." Before Cru could protest, Red waived him off. "I'm gonna grab the thirty-aught-six from the house for you. You stay here and throw off a couple of rounds every three or four minutes. Mix them up and move around a bit, so they think there's more than one of you. There's a game trail I hunt that heads about a hundred yards above their positions. Juan and I will work our way up there."

"How long you think it will take to get into position?" Cru asked.

"Probably about four to five hours." With that Red eased around back and went into the house. He came back with the hunting rifle, several loaded magazines, a water canteen, a two-way radio, and a bottle of Jack Daniels. "Everyone's in the safe room with the other two-way radio. Easy on the Jack, my friend, and wish us luck."

Chapter 36

Angelo Rossitello was elated. His arch enemy was dead, and Rossitello now figured to move in and take over much of the Dragna empire.

Detained with other business, Rafael Tijenera sent his most trusted lieutenant to meet with Rossitello and develop a plan to their mutual satisfaction. The meeting took place in a warehouse Rossitello leased near Los Angeles International Airport.

"I will concede to Rafael the drug business, but I should acquire all of the strip clubs and massage parlors. They were funded by my family back east and as such, they should stay within the family."

"Rafael don't care about la puta. We believe you could easily manage the prostitutes," Tijenera's lieutenant noted sarcastically. "But the horse gambling goes to us."

Rossitello wasn't so sure about that. "The trotters or the thoroughbreds?"

"When you are in the business of selling fish, do you not offer the salmon as well as the halibut?" the man asked.

"Race horses are a bit more complicated than fish."

"Rafael believes it necessary to control the whole business so as to justify the expense of the husbandry of horses."

The two negotiated for several hours. Rossitello and Tijenera's associate took notes during the course of their discussion. As they were wrapping up, two men wearing UPS uniforms and carrying packages entered the front of the large room. The bodyguards attending the meeting abruptly stopped them and took their packages away.

Startled, Rossitello yelled, "Take those packages outside. And get those fuckers the hell out of here."

Rossitello and Tijenera's associate sat watching as the guards ushered both men out of the building. As soon as they were alone, a man wearing a face mask appeared directly behind them. Before either man could react, the intruder grabbed the head of Tijenera's associate with one hand, came around front with the other, and sliced the man's throat from ear to ear with a large stiletto knife.

"Fuck!" Rossitello yelled as blood spraying from the mortally wounded man splattered his face, shirt, and all the paperwork on the small table. The masked assailant then calmly dropped the stiletto, turned around, and left.

* * *

Red and Juan worked their way around the foothills where the two attackers were positioned. They then made their way up the mountain through the thick brush and rock. Red hoped to pick up the game trail quickly so they could work their way above the assailants, without alerting them.

Every several minutes, Cru fired off a volley toward the position of the attackers. The attackers in turn fired a volley of large caliber bullets at him. Every now and then the attackers took potshots at the ranch house. The large caliber bullets smashed windows and punched huge holes in the siding. Keying the mic on his radio, Cru asked again, "You all okay in there?"

Christine answered, "We're still okay, but the bullets hitting the walls are terrifying the children. How much longer do you think this will last?"

"Hard to say. It might take them another three or four hours to get in position, maybe even all night." Cru remembered that in Vietnam the villagers would give the children betel nut to chew on and wrap clothing around their ears during attacks. "Try wrapping towels and stuff around the kid's ears," he advised.

As Cru hunkered down behind the large equipment by the ranch house, Red and Juan gradually worked their way to the top of the small mountain on the opposite side of the attackers' position.

"Here's the game trail," Red whispered. "Now we just have to follow it around. It should put us just above those two assholes."

Panting, Juan whispered back, "I don't think we make it before dark, Señor Red."

Red agreed. "No, we'll have to be very quiet when we get on the other side. We might have to wait until first light tomorrow to get a shot at them. Let's hope they haven't bugged out or changed position."

"I'm hungry," Juan noted.

"You eat almost as much as that damn Cru, Juan. We better keep going until we find our position. Here, have some jerky."

"Gracias, Señor Red."

* * *

Alton Deem was sitting at a blackjack table at Caesar's Palace in Las Vegas. He'd received a nice payoff for terminating Louie Dragna, and he wasted no time before splurging with the ample chunk of cash he had. He was celebrating with a prostitute who, though bored, humored the unpleasant man.

"Get me another beer, bitch," Deem ordered. The woman shot him a dirty look, but left to get the beer anyway. Before Deem's date returned, however, a pit boss and two large men approached him from behind.

"Mr. Deem?" the pit boss asked.

Deem looked at him with irritation, "Yeah, what do you want?"

"We've had some card counters in here recently, and by your actions on our camera we suspect you may be doing so as well."

"Fuck off!" Deem told him, while looking at the two

other men nervously.

At that, the pit boss shook his head and broke out into boisterous laughter. The two men grabbed Deem and forcefully ushered him away. Stunned, Deem could only babble in fear as he was brought into one of the casino back rooms and unceremoniously tossed on the floor. Watching all three men apprehensively, Deem slowly rose to his feet and brushed off his clothes. In a short time, three more men came into the room.

"I want my lawyer," Deem whined.

"You aren't under arrest, Mr. Deem. By the way, do you like scenic overlooks?"

"What the fuck do you care?" Deem didn't understand what he was getting at.

A back door opened and the three men ushered Deem into a waiting vehicle. They drove out to Hoover Dam, and everyone got out of the vehicle and stood by the bridge overlooking the dam. Sensing what was coming, Deem started sobbing. "No, don't...please, I'll do anything you want, tell you anything you want," he pleaded.

Unfortunately for Deem, the only thing these men wanted was to see him suffer. One of the men casually took out a large stiletto and cut off a piece of Deem's right ear. Deem screamed in pain, while covering what was left of his badly bleeding ear.

"How much did you get for killing Louie Dragna?" the man demanded.

"They made me do it. Tijenera and Rossitello made me do it!"

"Where's Tijenera hiding?" the man asked.

"I don't know, honest to God, I don't know. If I did, I'd take you right to the sonofabitch!" The man with the knife nodded to one of the other men, who put a noose around Deem's neck.

"No...no!" Deem screamed in vain.

Two men held the noose while they all wrestled the

screaming, kicking Deem over the edge of the dam. Soon only the two men holding the rope prevented Deem from falling to his death. Deem choked and sputtered, grasping the rope above his head in an attempt to save himself from suffocating. After a short time, the men dragged Deem back up. As they pulled him up, his bowels let go and he filled his pants.

With two men holding the rope and two men holding Deem by the shoulders, the man asked again, "You know where Tijenera is now, asshole?"

Barely audible, Deem croaked, "No, I don't know anything. I don't even know who you are."

"Well, that ain't right, Deem. You should know the name of the man who kills you. I'm Billy. Billy Falconnetti." Falconnetti cut the rope and nodded to the other men who released their grip. Deem tumbled down the side of the dam, his piercing screams echoing throughout the canyon until he plunged into the turbulent water below.

Chapter 37

At first light, Red and Juan worked themselves into position above the two men who were attacking the ranch. They were almost two hundred yards directly above the two and could see the large caliber barrels protruding from the sniper nests the men had thrown together.

Red grabbed Juan's arm and whispered, "You stay here and when I give you the signal, fire at that barrel sticking out."

"What if they don't come out?" Juan asked.

"We fire a couple volleys at them and believe me, they'll get nervous and pop their heads out like turtles. Wait for my signal. We have to kind of hurry now. Otherwise Cru might shoot our asses."

Red worked his way above the other man's position. After sighting his weapon, he waived to Juan. Both men opened up on the gun barrels below them.

The man below Red screamed in pain as his gun was wrenched out of his hands by Red's M-16 fire. The other man pulled his gun in and held tight. After several minutes, the barrel of the man below Juan reappeared and Red signaled Juan to start firing again. Red fired again at the position directly under him, kicking up dirt and vegetation. As predicted, after several minutes the man slowly eased his head out and looked up, trying to see who was shooting at them. As soon as Red was certain he had a clean shot, he fired once, hitting the man square in the forehead and killing him instantly.

When he saw his accomplice tumble out of his hide dead, the second man lost his nerve and shouted, "I give up! Don't shoot. I give up!"

"Throw your gun out and step out with both hands in the air," Red shouted back. The long barreled rifle was tossed out of the hide.

"Throw everything out or fucking die," Red ordered. A large handgun flew out, followed by a hunting knife. Then the man stepped out with his hands over his head.

"Cover me, Juan." As Juan trained his rifle on the man, Red cautiously worked his way down toward the man. "Don't shoot, Cru!" he shouted down at the ranch house.

When he reached the attacker, Red ordered, "On your stomach, asshole." The man slowly got down on all fours and stretched his hands out. Red picked up the knife, handgun, and rifle and signaled Juan to come down. They tied the man's hands behind his back and started toward the house.

"We got 'em, Cru. We're coming down. Don't shoot anymore."

Cru had been anxiously waiting to hear the outcome. "Got it, Red. Come on down!" He headed into the house and reported to the women and children. "But I want you to stay in the safe room until we give the all clear. They're coming down, but anything could happen."

Christine embraced him. "We'll stay put. But can you bring us some orange juice and candy bars?"

Soon Red, Juan, and their captive reached the barn where Cru stood waiting for them, gun in hand. "What are we gonna do with this piece of shit?"

Juan had an idea about that. "I take care of him." They had never torn down the old chicken coop where Juan was detained, so he marched the man over there, pushed him inside, and shackled him by his hands and feet. He put a jug of water within reach.

"You can't leave me here. I'll die of heat stroke," the

man protested.

"That would be my hope, Señor," Juan said as he headed out the door.

* * *

With Lieutenant Dooley's assistance, Arnold Redmond and Andrew Crucianelli were brought in safely and now sat before a legal hearing conducted by the state of California. The events of the past eighteen month gang war were at issue.

Prosecuting attorneys sought to assign responsibility for the deadly war to Redmond and Crucianelli, pointing out that they were the catalyst for the whole episode. Defending attorneys claimed that Redmond and Crucianelli were simply pawns, used by powerful gangs to boost their own agendas.

The trial received ample publicity and was well attended by members of the press. Many character witnesses had been brought forth on behalf of the two accused men, and the hearing was now in the fifth day of deliberation. The last character witness was Victor Manual Lopez. Lopez was a member of the 1st Cavalry unit in Vietnam that helped deliver Cru, Red, and the other remaining survivors of their ordeal in the bush, into safety.

"Mr. Lopez, you are familiar with the two defendants in this hearing, are you not?" the defense attorney began.

"Yes."

"Can you tell us how you came to know Andrew Crucianelli and Arnold Redmond?"

"I met them in Vietnam when they had been targeted for death by a black market operation."

"And you helped those men. You were among the members of the First Cavalry unit who saved their lives, is that not true?"

Lopez nodded. "I was involved."

The defense attorney continued. "As I understand it, the man charged with the attempted murder of these two, and the actual murder of several others as well as a smuggler of drugs and weapons, is a former United States Air Force Master Sergeant named Howard McKay, is that correct?"

"That is correct, but he might have been the only sane one among us," Lopez added.

In further quizzing by the defense attorney, Lopez testified to the honesty and integrity of the two men in question, detailing their courage under fire and their initiative in eradicating the drug smuggling operations.

When the defense attorney finished, the prosecuting attorney rose and approached the witness box.

Looking around the courtroom he said, "Mr. Lopez, if I'm not mistaken, you implied that Howard McKay was justified in the activities he pursued?"

"You are mistaken," Lopez replied. "I said McKay might have been one of the few sane people in the war."

Sensing an opening the prosecutor continued, "So you support McKay's activities of murder, drug smuggling, and mayhem."

The courtroom, filled with witnesses, attorneys, police authorities, and members of the press, now sat silent, awaiting Lopez's reply.

"You're twisting my words, counselor. I said no such thing."

"But you said—"

Before the prosecuting attorney could finish, Lopez raised his voice and interrupted. "I said McKay might have been right."

"Can you please explain that," the attorney pressed.

Lopez looked directly at him and very clearly stated, "McKay might have been the only sane one among us."

A murmur went through the room as members of the jury, the press, and others present reacted to Lopez's seemingly outlandish claim.

"Order! Order, please." The judge banged his gavel.

"You will continue your explanation, Mr. Lopez."

Lopez slowly looked around the room. "Do you think anything we're doing over there makes a bit of difference?" He paused briefly, then continued. "Do you think anything we do is of any benefit to the poor bastards we're supposed to be helping?"

Lopez paused again. "In World War II, we helped throw out the Japanese, who had replaced the French as the Vietnamese masters. Then we let the French back in. And when the Vietnamese asked us for help in throwing out the despotic French masters, we took up for the French!"

Again, there was murmuring in the court until the attorney interrupted. "What are you saying? Are you saying the United States was wrong to intervene on behalf of the French and South Vietnamese authorities?"

"That's bullshit," Lopez said with conviction.

"I will have to ask you to clarify your remark, Mr. Lopez," the judge advised.

"Bullshit!" Lopez said again, only this time louder, and then continued. "On whose behalf did we really intervene? Was it really the Vietnamese? Or was it the automobile conglomeration who wanted cheap Vietnamese rubber and access to offshore minerals and resources?"

One of the prosecuting attorneys interrupted. "Your Honor, this has nothing to do with the issue at hand."

The judge waived him off. "We will hear Mr. Lopez's testimony. It is the very least we can do, considering that this man served valiantly in Vietnam and provided assistance with the removal of a man who abused his position for profit. Please go on, Mr. Lopez."

Lopez nodded. "Thank you, Your Honor. Let me ask this. Who benefits from our presence in Vietnam? Perhaps the war profiteers who are able to sell the United States military tons of C-rations left over from World War II, often causing sickness in the men who have to eat them."

Looking around, Lopez paused again. "Or perhaps

all those munitions and weapons manufacturers who need new markets for their goods and a new testing ground for their effectiveness."

The people in the room sat silently, riveted by the testimony of a hero who for some reason had gone sour on his country.

Lopez wasn't finished. "Who else benefits? The list goes on. Perhaps it's that gang of unscrupulous bankers who make hundreds of millions of dollars in illegal currency manipulation. Or maybe the hundreds of civilian contractors who make huge profits gaming the system. Or how about the chemical manufacturers who create new poisons, which are sprayed down upon the very people we were sent to help, not to mention our own troops. It appears now as if McKay was simply doing the American thing..."

Lopez sat silent for a moment, allowing the room to take in what he had told them. But he had more to say. "You think anyone really gives a shit what's happening over there?" Pointing at the two GIs on trial, he said, "No one gives a shit what happened to them...or the damn Vietnamese either, for that matter. Right now, as we sit here, the United States is dropping thousands of tons of bombs from supersonic aircraft on a people who still plow their fields with oxen! And right now, as we speak, we are spraying poison on the crops of people who are already starving."

A reporter interrupted before the judge could silence him. "No, there must be more. There has to be more to justify the madness!"

Watching him, Lopez slowly shook his head. He again pointed to Redmond and Crucianelli and addressed the room. "When their old wounds hurt so badly they are forced to cry, do you think anyone gives a shit? When they wake up in the middle of the night in terror because of some horror they witnessed, do you think anyone cares?"

He then pointed toward the room's large picture windows, from which the busy midday hustle and bustle could be seen. As if on cue, a group of business men in suits emerged from a restaurant across the street, laughing and joking. "You think they give a rat's ass?" Lopez asked. "McKay and others like him knew the answer. They knew the answer all too well." Lopez's voice trailed off. "They knew that nobody gives a shit. In that respect, McKay was right."

The court room was now silent. People turned their heads down and away, stunned and saddened. Several women sniffled.

Taking a breath, the judge said, "Your testimony will be placed under consideration, Mr. Lopez. You may now step down. This hearing is adjourned until ten o'clock tomorrow morning."

All eyes were on Victor Manual Lopez as he stepped down and walked away.

* * *

"All rise," the bailiff intoned as the presiding judge strode into the court room.

"Please be seated," the judge advised, looking around the court room. "Ladies and gentlemen, this is a very unusual case we've heard this week. We have a whole series of crimes, resulting from the ill advised actions of these two men. Two men, somewhat embittered, who returned from the cauldron of war to an unwelcoming country. Two men who decided to take action against what they saw as the scourge of our nation."

The judge took a long look at Redmond and Crucianelli who sat stone faced before him. "I could punish these men to the full extent of the law, and no one could fault me. But I will not. Though it was not their intention, these men toppled two organized crime families and took the wind out of the sails of a notorious drug gang. Their cooperation with the police, in the form of Lieutenant Dooley, also rooted out corrupt elements in our own police force and judicial system, the ramifications of which will be felt for years.

169

I will not punish these men any further than they already have been, in their short lives. Their sentence will be limited to three years of parole. However, as a condition of the parole, if I so much as hear of a jaywalking violation on the part of Mr. Crucianelli or Mr. Redmond they will incur the full wrath of this vengeful old judge. Case dismissed!"

The courtroom erupted in shouts and cheers, as the bailiff led the two men out of the courtroom.

Epilogue

Doug Montrell and many other friends and relatives of Cru and Red were now attending a gathering at the ranch.

"This is a beautiful place," Doug Montrell commented.

"It is," Dooley agreed. He had brought his young family out and was now watching his son frolic in the pool with Juan's children.

"Congratulations on your promotion, by the way," Montrell added. For his part in clearing up the gang war, and taking down corrupt elements in the department, Dooley was promoted to captain and given complete responsibility for the gang unit.

"Thanks, Doug. I'm glad your friends came out of this relatively unscathed."

"They were damned lucky," Montrell acknowledged.

Victor Manual Lopez also was in attendance. Lopez and Dooley had become acquainted through a veteran's group they belonged to. Lopez had been quietly working behind the scenes with Dooley, regarding the dilemma their mutual friends had become entangled in.

Juan's son, Abel watched the younger children as they threw the ball in the pool. He had recovered from his wounds and was now attending the university. With the scholarship that Red and Cru set up for him in the name of their late friend Domingo, he was free to use his summers helping around the ranch. He planned on continuing straight through to law school, and before long, he would be studying for his LSATs. With Abel's help, Juan had completed the large ranch house and barn and even added a swimming pool.

While some guests lounged at the pool, others milled around, admiring the beautiful home and surroundings. Crucianelli's parents, along with his Aunt Tesla and Redmond's mother were among those at the gathering. Christine was showing them her herb garden.

"I just love the smell of fresh basil," Mrs. Crucianelli said. "Can you grow it here year round?"

"Just about," Christine said. "The problem is the excessive sun and heat during the day, not to mention the occasional freezes at night. I've learned where to put the plants to optimize shade and wind blocks."

Later in the evening, Crucianelli, Redmond, and Montrell sat drinking beer and watching the sun set on the mesa.

"You guys gonna stay out here, I take it?" Montrell asked.

"Could do a lot worse," Redmond told him.

"Hey, we got plenty of room in the Red Crew Inn," Crucianelli hinted. He had so named the large ranch house, with all its amenities.

"I still have a little time left with Uncle Sam. Don't think I should go AWOL just yet. Although you guys probably think I need to go to jail, just so I don't feel left out."

"Why don't you think about joining us here when you're done. Unless you plan on reenlisting, that is. I understand, if you do; stateside duty must be so exciting for you," Cru teased.

Red agreed. "We could use the help out here, Monty. The construction company Juan started has enough business to keep five men going, five and a half if you count Cru."

Montrell got into the spirit of things. "Are you trying to tell me Cru doesn't do the work of five men all by himself?"

"Oh, he'll do the work of five men, all right, if four of them are over eighty and the fifth one is missing both legs," Red replied.

"You guys just don't appreciate the finer aspects of management," Cru said. "My job is to ensure that those around me fulfill their tasks to the best of their abilities."

"When you're on the job, those around you have to fulfill every task," Red corrected.

"I'm gonna go see if there's any ribs left," Cru said. "I'll let Juan know you're out here. He'll probably have to carry you back to your bunks after you pass out."

"Leave the ribs on the horses alone. They're still alive and might need 'em," Red called out to Cru's retreating back.

Montrell laughed and shook his head. "Good to be with you boys, again. Good to be with you."

www.ingramcontent.com/pod-product-compliance
Lightning Source LLC
Chambersburg PA
CBHW071215260626
47162CB00004B/1300

* 9 7 8 1 9 4 3 2 6 7 1 1 8 *